THE FREEDOM FINDERS
Break Your Chains

EMILY CONOLAN

ALLEN&UNWIN
SYDNEY·MELBOURNE·AUCKLAND·LONDON

First published by Allen & Unwin in 2018

Copyright © Text, Emily Conolan 2018
Copyright © Cover illustration, Sher Rill Ng 2018
Copyright © Interview replies on pages 263–268, Theresa Sainty 2018

The author claims no ownership over any Tasmanian Aboriginal cultural material referenced in the story, including palawa kani language words or the important cultural practice of shell necklace making.

Tasmanian Aboriginal cultural material used with permission from Theresa Sainty. With thanks to the Tasmanian Aboriginal Corporation for use of the palawa kani language word 'Waylitja'. palawa kani is the revived Tasmanian Aboriginal language.

Every effort has been made to ensure that, at the time of publication, information in this book pertaining to Tasmanian Aboriginal cultural references is correct. Please contact the publisher with any concerns.

All rights reserved. No part of this book may be reproduced or transmitted in any form or by any means, electronic or mechanical, including photocopying, recording or by any information storage and retrieval system, without prior permission in writing from the publisher. The Australian *Copyright Act 1968* (the Act) allows a maximum of one chapter or ten per cent of this book, whichever is the greater, to be photocopied by any educational institution for its educational purposes provided that the educational institution (or body that administers it) has given a remuneration notice to the Copyright Agency (Australia) under the Act.

Allen & Unwin
83 Alexander Street
Crows Nest NSW 2065
Australia
Phone: (61 2) 8425 0100
Email: info@allenandunwin.com
Web: www.allenandunwin.com

A catalogue record for this book is available from the National Library of Australia

ISBN 978 1 76029 491 5

For teaching resources,
explore www.allenandunwin.com/resources/for-teachers

Cover design by Karen Scott and Sandra Nobes
Text design by Sandra Nobes and Karen Scott
Set in 11.5 pt Sabon by Sandra Nobes
Photo of Theresa Sainty on page 263 © Charles Chadwick
Vintage map on pages 280–281 © Lukasz Szwaj/Shutterstock
Photo of Emily Conolan on page 284 © Nick Tompson
This book was printed in Australia in January 2018 by McPherson's Printing Group

10 9 8 7 6 5 4 3 2 1

www.emilyconolan.com.au

The paper in this book is FSC® certified. FSC® promotes environmentally responsible, socially beneficial and economically viable management of the world's forests.

To Anwen, Ben, and all those
who call Tasmania home

WARNING: YOU MAY DIE WHILE READING THIS BOOK.

When you read this book, *you* are the main character, and *you* make the choices that direct the story.

At the end of many chapters, you will face life-and-death decisions. Turn to the page directed by your choice, and keep reading.

Some of these decisions may not work out well for you. But there is a happy ending...somewhere.

In the Freedom Finder series, it is your quest to find freedom through the choices you make. If you reach a dead end, turn back to the last choice you made, and find a way through.

NEVER GIVE UP. GOOD LUCK.

AUTHOR'S NOTE

DEAR READER,

Let me tell you something very personal. My ancestors left England and arrived here – in Tasmania, previously known as Van Diemen's Land, before that known as Lutruwita – when the presence of Europeans in this land was still very new.

In 1825, when this book is set, Tasmanian Aboriginal people had already been here for at least forty thousand years. My ancestors on my mother's side had been here exactly two years. That makes me seventh-generation Tasmanian, something that people boast about these days, but my family has been here for just a pinprick of time compared to the First Nations Australians.

When I came to write this book, I had to face the uncomfortable truth that my ancestors' home in Bothwell was built on stolen land. The violence, dispossession and disease that came about as a result of Australia's colonisation (invasion by white people) is touched upon in this book, and in the fact files at the back. And my family played a part in that.

In writing this book, I had to dig inside myself and pull out some of the messy feelings I have about being Tasmanian. I also had to ask myself: *To what extent is it okay to show young readers the kind of racism and offensive attitudes people held in 1825?*

By including racist scenes and words in my book, I don't want to help continue or spread racism. In the story, characters call Aboriginal people 'natives'; suggest Aboriginal people need to be violently attacked in order to 'teach them a lesson'; and show religious intolerance towards a Muslim man. That behaviour was not okay in 1825, and it is not okay now. I also didn't want to cause hurt to any Aboriginal or non-Anglo readers, who I worried might feel upset to see those racist views in print.

But in the end, I decided it would be more hurtful to leave out the racism and pretend it never happened. Because racist words and actions *did* happen, and are still happening today, and it's impossible to deal with a problem that no one will talk about. I also like to think that, since this is a book where *you* choose what happens next, readers like yourself might go back and forth and try out all the different scenes – including those concerning Waylitja, the fictional Aboriginal character in this story – and see how those choices work out for you and for the other characters.

Waylitja has the most beautiful name, meaning 'parrot'. I have the wonderful Theresa Sainty to thank for that, as she named him. Theresa, a Tasmanian Aboriginal Elder, was my main cultural advisor on this story, generously sharing her time and knowledge to help make it better. See the back of the book for an interview with her.

After colonisation, the Aboriginal languages of Tasmania were left in tatters. Theresa has played a big role in bringing all the fragments of language together, to create palawa kani, a beautiful and rich language that Tasmanian Aboriginal people can use today. (See tacinc.com.au/programs/palawa-kani for more information, including the permission policy for the use of palawa kani words.)

My huge thanks go to Theresa, and to the Tasmanian Aboriginal Corporation, for giving me permission to use Waylitja's name and other cultural material in the story.

My gratitude also goes to Ruth Langford, Tony Brown, Denise Robinson and Tony Burgess for their time and encouragement, and to Aboriginal cultural consultant extraordinaire Lisa Fuller for her editorial advice. I'd also like to recognise that this book is set on the lands of the Muwinina people (Hobart) and the people whose country encompassed the Bothwell area and offer my deepest respect for and acknowledgement of their countries and these Elders both past and present.

I'm lucky that I've never had to fight for my freedom in the extreme way that many of the characters in this series are forced to do. Everyone in this book is searching for their own kind of freedom, and not everyone finds it. However, through my work as a refugee advocate setting up the Tasmanian Asylum Seeker Support and as a TAFE teacher, I've met many people from all over the world whose lives *have* tested them in this way, and their stories were what inspired me to write this series of books.

In real life, the choices that are laid out in front of us are more blurry, more unpredictable, and more complex than those shown in this series. (And real people don't have the option of flipping back a few pages and trying a different choice!) But I hope that it will lead you to think about what freedom means to you and how far you might go to achieve it – and to think about how the people you see all around you are, in fact, Freedom Finders.

Because humans *are* Freedom Finders – that's just what we do. That's why we migrate, why we begin new jobs or families or relationships, why we try new things, or have dreams, or reach out to others. That search for freedom often plays an important role in why we make the choices that we do. We are all searching for whatever makes us feel free in our hearts.

I hope that you enjoy the journey.

EMILY CONOLAN, 2018

PROLOGUE

You squeal with delight. You are three years old, it is 1815 in Kilkenny, Ireland, and it's the first time you've sat astride a horse. You feel her hot, wide body breathing beneath you.

'Shall we make her walk, then?' asks Da.

Just then a shout comes from the master. 'Ryan! That's my finest mare! What the hell do you think you're doing?'

Da slips you down from the horse's back and sends you running home to Ma, for he doesn't want you to see him be whipped by the master. He doesn't want you to know, yet, that this is the way things are for Irish folk like you.

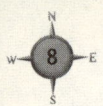

YOU'RE SEVEN, AND Da's working for a different master now. One golden afternoon, he brings home a horse: an old mare, whiskery around the mouth, that he's talked the master into letting him keep now she's considered useless.

Your ma curses your da's lack of sense – 'Where are we going to keep her? How will we afford the food?' – but you and your older sister, Erin, will love this mare till her dying days. You will plait her tail and check her hooves for stones like Da shows you, and learn to ride bareback, and you will cry for days when she reaches the end of her life a year later and goes to horse heaven.

YOU'RE TEN YEARS old. Erin would have turned eighteen, but she died last year in childbirth. The baby died too. Most Irish families are large, but your ma had 'women's troubles', and now you're the only child left.

Da is away a lot. You're not sure why; he's secretive about it. But then one night he has a bit to drink, and he tells you everything: how he fought in the Irish Rebellion of 1798, and how he's now working on forming a new secret society of Irishmen

to free Ireland from English rule. 'We'll be our own masters!' he tells you. He's a hero in your eyes.

IT IS 1825 and you're thirteen years old. Last year, Da was caught setting fire to an English government ship. Soldiers took him away to a prison hulk somewhere on the River Thames in London. His case still hasn't been heard in court.

After he was taken, you and Ma also left dear, green Ireland for the crowded, cobbled roads of London. Even now, a year on, you watch the horses clopping by, their carriages carrying fancy Englishmen, and you miss Ireland, and Da, and the horses terribly. You miss the sweet grassy smell of horse-breath, and the bright-blue skies.

You and Ma found a one-room hovel in a London slum. The rats are fatter than you are. The idea of freedom for Ireland seems a distant, shiny, imaginary thing, like a soap-bubble carried on the wind. You can barely keep it in sight – but you know that you must. For Da.

✦ Go to page 10.

10

There's a clatter and a scream. A wooden crack splits the air, and everyone in the narrow street whips around as if a musket's been shot. You see it all in an instant: a carriage with a snapped axle, tilting dangerously to one side; the carriage-driver, bruised and bloody, thrown to the ground; and amid the chaos, wild and angry as a giant, the horse, rearing up on his back legs and neighing in panic.

Mothers snatch their babies away, and little boys in braces and caps run out of their houses to look. Someone is helping the carriage driver to press a towel to the wound on his head, but no one knows how to settle the horse; a couple of people are shouting and waving their arms, trying to frighten him into submission, but they are making things worse.

You don't know what you're going to do, or how – you only know that this is your moment to act. That big wild beast is only frightened because he's trapped; because everything he knows just turned upside down. You know how he feels.

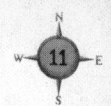

The horse is all teeth and eyeballs, his hooves rising and falling like threshing hammers, but you dart through the chaos, right underneath the horse, ignoring cries of 'Stop!' and 'You want to get yourself killed, girl?' until you can touch his sweaty chest. His breath is coming hot and fast through his flared nostrils, and his heart is pounding like a bodhran drum.

'Whoa, boy,' you say. 'Easy there... easy there, boy.'

Right now, it feels as though your da is here beside you: guiding your hands as you stroke the horse's flanks; showing you how to loosen the straps that have tangled around his neck; telling you to watch how the horse's ears are swivelling towards you, listening to your voice as his panic subsides.

'Easy there...' you soothe, and the horse drops his head so you can scratch him behind the ears. The crowd breaks into astonished applause. The horse bristles at the sudden sound, but settles again as you whisper to him and pat his big, hairy nose.

The carriage door opens and the crowd gasps: there has been a lady trapped inside the whole time! People rush forward to help her down. She is wearing a flowered hat and robes of blue silk.

Incredibly, she does not seem angry or frightened but is smiling and nodding her thanks.

The lady's eyes fall on you. Without saying a word, she walks up to you and takes one of your small, grubby hands in hers. Her hands are pale pink, like the roses you sometimes see the barrow-lady selling, with delicate, long fingers that have clearly never been blistered by scalding-hot washing tubs or callused by hefting a spade.

'How did you manage to calm the horse?' she asks you. To your surprise, her accent is Irish, like your own.

'My da showed me how,' you murmur. 'Back when we lived in Ireland.'

'Ah, a fellow Irish girl.' The lady smiles broadly. 'Do you miss our homeland?'

'How can I not, ma'am?' you confess.

'It is the best place on God's earth,' she agrees. 'My heart yearns for it too. You were very brave just now – do you know that?'

You shrug and smile. The people on the street are going back to their everyday business, but the hum and clatter of London seems to have faded around you, and when you look into this Irishwoman's eyes, you feel as though you're held inside a bubble of

time – as though she sees something more in you than a barefoot, homesick child.

'I was just like you when I arrived here,' she tells you tenderly. 'I had no idea how to survive. But I can see already that you're smart, and brave, and that you have a good heart. If you follow it, I'm sure you'll find your way.'

Your eyes fill with tears. Kindness is such a rare thing in your life. You hadn't let yourself admit how thirsty you were for it until now.

'I...don't know how to help my da,' you say haltingly. You wipe away your tears fiercely. 'He's in prison. He was trying to make Ireland free, and—'

The lady gasps. 'Then I know that your da must be a hero,' she says. 'We must fight together, my darling, and never give up. Here.' She slips something from her wrist and puts it into your hand. 'Keep this, close and secret. Only use it when you must. When you understand its meaning, you'll know it's time to pass it on.'

You look down. Nestled in your palm is a golden bracelet set with seven coloured gemstones. One's as dark-green as a fir tree. The next is black as the night sky, and another clear and bright as a star. Two are emerald-green, like the Irish grass. One's a ruby, red as blood. The seventh stone seems to hold all of these colours swirled together: an impossibly beautiful rainbow that shimmers in the light with a bluish fire.

'Do you mean me to keep this, ma'am?' you ask incredulously, raising your head. You can't believe that such a beautiful thing could belong to you. But the lady has gone.

You slip the bracelet into your pocket. Suddenly you're certain that you can survive here – *will* survive here. You feel as light and mad and wondrous as one of those hot-air balloons you've heard can sail the skies.

YOU RUN HOME, bursting to tell Ma your news. As you bang the door closed behind you, the room goes dark. Ma hasn't lit a lamp or started cooking, as she usually would have. Where is she? The only sound is your own breath, still loud and fast from running.

Then you notice the stink in the room, sweaty and fetid. You open the door a crack, and a strip of dusky light falls across the room. In the corner where Ma sleeps, a heap of blankets rises and falls.

'Ma?' You run to her, pull back the blankets and let out a cry. All the happiness slips out of your heart like an egg that's just been cracked.

Ma hasn't been feeling well for a few days, but now her sleeping face is covered in blisters, and you know: it's the smallpox. *Dear God, Jesus, Mary and Joseph, not that.*

You get busy immediately, shaking out the blankets and smoothing them over your ma more comfortably, and putting water on to boil for a soup to feed her when she wakes.

She stirs and calls your name in a hoarse voice. You're by her side in an instant, holding a cup of water to her cracked lips.

'You're going to be all right, Ma,' you assure her, hoping she won't notice the tremble in your voice. 'Danny O'Reilly, he...well, he had what you have, and he's fit as a fiddle now.'

Your ma manages a weak smile. Both of you know that Danny was one of the only people back home in Kilkenny to survive the last outbreak of smallpox, which took the lives of dozens of others. But where there's life, you reason, there's hope. There must be.

'I want you to go and stay with Mrs Raeburn down the road,' she whispers. 'If it's my time to go,

then may the Lord take me home – but it's not your time. I can't have you catching it too.'

'But Ma,' you burst out, 'who's going to look after you?'

'Just go till I'm better,' she whispers. 'I can take care of myself all right.'

Your ma can barely stand up – so how's she going to take care of herself if you go? *No way*, you think. *I'm here for her, smallpox be damned*. But then again, you reason, you're not going to be of much help to her if you catch it too. At least if you stay healthy, you can bring in a little money, sell your bracelet if need be, help her to stay off her feet a while longer while she recovers. *If she recovers*.

Ma's eyes have closed again. You settle yourself down on the floor beside her to think, and while you are thinking, you unpick the hem of your petticoat and slip the bracelet into the hem, then sew it back up. Whatever comes next, you know that you must follow the lady's instructions: keep it close. Keep it secret. Only use it when you must – and don't give it up until you understand its true meaning... whatever that is.

Perhaps there's a cure for the smallpox here in London, you think wildly, knowing deep down that

if there were, you'd have heard of it. *One that only the rich can buy. I can sell this bracelet to save Ma – that can be its purpose!* Your mind is like a sparrow trapped indoors, beating at the windows for a way out.

Your ma opens her blue eyes, the same summer-sky shade as your own. She seems to have summoned some of her fighting spirit, because she props herself up on one elbow. 'Out with you,' she says fiercely. 'Down the street to Mrs Raeburn's – that's an order! Now go, you damn foolish girl!'

But you can see she's shaking with the effort, and there's a tearing feeling in your heart that you know too well: the same feeling you had when Erin died; when they took Da away. The feeling of grief rolling in like a storm.

✦ If you leave to stay with Mrs Raeburn and look for a cure, go to page 31.
✦ If you stay to care for your ma, despite the risk of catching smallpox yourself, go to page 18.
✦ To read a fact file on smallpox, turn to page 253, then return to this page to make your choice.

You grit your teeth. You're not used to defying your ma, but you know it's the right thing to do.

'Don't be daft,' you tell her. 'You're weak as a cat, and I'm staying here. I'm putting on some soup.'

Your ma collapses back on the bed, too drained to fight you. Your little one-room home fills with the smell of boiling onions – almost good enough to drown out the stench of the nearby cesspools and the stink of your ma's sweaty skin.

Dinner isn't much, just onion, salt, water and a little potato. Ma manages to drink a bit before slipping back into sleep. Her breath, and the sound of passing horses' hooves, become the only sounds to be heard on this damp night.

It's not long after dinner, as you scrub the pot, that you begin to feel a little strange. The first thing that you notice is that your back's throbbing, as though you've been carrying bricks all day. Then a headache starts up at the back of

your head, as if someone has slammed an axe into it. The last thing you remember thinking is, *I'm so cold…*

You wake up staring at the water-stained ceiling of your home. Your throat feels enormous. You're on the floor… how did you get onto the floor? The fire's gone out. It hurts to roll over.

'Erin,' you moan. 'Erin?'

Erin's gone, some dim part of your brain tells you. *She died in childbirth, remember?* You don't want to remember. You just want to sleep.

A hundred flies are landing on you, and their feet are on fire. Your skin is erupting and swelling like sticky pudding on a burning pot. Dirt and drizzle, ash and prickles… the maid is in the parlour, eating bread and honey. Day, night, dim, bright. You're so hot, your throat is a burnt field. Blackbirds baked in a pie.

You awaken who knows how much later to the sound of rocks being thrown against your door.

'Get away from it, Jimmy, or I'll tan your hide!' screeches a voice.

'Aw, there's no harm in it, Ma – they're dead. She and her ma both. Me and Douglas peeked in and saw them. Dead as dormice, they are!'

'And you want to be dead too? No? Then stay away from there!'

There is one last rock – *bang* – and then footsteps patter away. It's cold. You look around, bewildered. You see a dried-up patch of scum on the floor and vaguely remember vomiting. Your body is stiff as an old rag, and your skin – oh, dear God, it looks like someone has been walking up and down your body with red-hot nails sticking from their boots. It hurts to breathe, but you are alive, and the fever has passed, so it seems you will live.

Ma?

Panic flashes through you, sudden as lightning. You crawl to her. She's rigid as a board, and cold.

You pull the blanket up over your ma's face, feeling giddy and numb, your heartbeat pounding in your ears. You notice the scrubbing brush still in the pot. You can't take in any more. All the blood feels as though it's swirling away from your head. Your limbs start to tingle, and you faint on the floor.

You wake at dawn to somebody pounding on your door. 'Open up! That's an order!'

You get to your feet, feeling stronger than before. Just before you make it to the door, though, you hear the same voice say, 'Seems they're right –

nobody alive in there. Same as the last house, poor blighters.'

You open the door to the astonished face of a constable who was, it seems, preparing to break your door down with one shoulder.

'I'm alive,' you croak, watching the horror spread over his face as he takes in the sight of you. 'Ma's dead, though.'

A lump rises in your throat as you say it aloud for the first time. *May the Lord take me home*, you remember her voice saying, and tears prick at your eyes.

'You're naught but a child,' he observes. 'Where's the rest of your family?'

You hang your head. 'I only had the one sister, and she died. My da's in prison. He's a good man, though,' you add hastily. 'He just—'

'He's pure as the virgin snow, I'm sure,' drawls the constable. You're not sure what he means by that, but you don't like the tone of his voice. 'Right then, milady, it's off to the poorhouse with you.'

'What?' Shock floods your veins. You've heard rumours of the poorhouses, packed to the rafters with orphans, the unwanted human detritus of London: they're not much more than storage houses

for cheap labour, and they're pits of crime and disease. 'I can't go there! I'm staying here!'

'Like hell you are. This property don't belong to you, miss, and you don't have a choice in the matter.'

But that's the thing – you *do* have a choice. It wasn't your choice to survive the smallpox, nor your ma's to die from it, but you've got your life now, and where there's life, you tell yourself again, there's hope. There must be.

✦ If you shut the door in the constable's face and lock him out, go to page 23.

✦ If you try to slip past the constable and into the street, go to page 25.

Bang! You slam the door in the constable's face before you have enough time to think about the world of trouble you might get into. This is your home, and no one's going to take it from you.

You hear a roar, and look down to see four fat, pink fingers wedged in the door. The constable must have put his hand out to stop you, and you have slammed the door shut on it. You're in for it now.

There is a splintering crash as he kicks the door open, and you retreat to the corner of the room as he advances on you, his face pink as a boiled ham, clasping his broken fingers and swearing like a trooper.

'You bloody vermin! Poorhouse too good for you, eh? Thought you'd prefer a quick trip with a short stop? That's what you'll get, then, and may the devil take you!'

Your heart is in your mouth – he means to hang you by the neck! In front of all those onlookers at the gallows, who watch and jeer and laugh.

With his good hand, the constable grabs you by the collar. You wriggle, but he's too strong. 'Take me to the poorhouse, please!' you beg. Even there would be better than gaol.

'Too late for that now,' snarls the constable. 'But you won't have to worry, my pet,' he goes on. 'They tie the ladies' legs together before they fall, so that no one can see your knickers flashing while you kick and die like a fish on a hook! Oh, it'll be a proper dignified death you're going to, for assaulting a constable at work!'

The last thing you see as you're dragged from your home is Ma's body lying covered on the bed, and right now you almost wish you'd died of smallpox in your own home too – better than the terrifying prospect of the gallows in front of Newgate Prison.

✦ In this matter you have no choice. Go to page 65.

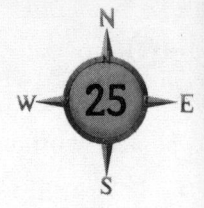

You duck, and then wriggle past the constable's knee and through the doorway, dodging his thick arms. The constable blows a shrill whistle behind you and gives chase. Your bare feet slap the cobblestones, and some local boys laugh and point as you streak down the street. You're still weak from the smallpox, but you're amazed at how fast you can go once fear starts pumping through your veins.

As you glance behind you, you hear a soft *thump* and your world goes white. Suddenly, you are lying on the ground, entangled in somebody's wet washing. You hear angry shrieks from the washerwoman and the huffing of the guard as he closes in on you and grabs you by the scruff of your neck. The local boys are laughing fit to wet themselves. You murder them with your eyes as you are dragged away.

You feel small as an ant as you are led up to the face of the poorhouse, which towers above you like a red cliff, its small windows reflecting the grey sheen of the sky.

You're thrown into a room with some other young

women, who sit around a pile of old rope, unrolling and teasing out the fibres with their fingertips. Some of them have a blank look in their eyes, as if they've lived a thousand years on earth and nothing would surprise them anymore. Others seem bright and almost obstinately cheerful, commenting and laughing as they work. They've still got a bit of the fighting spirit in them, Ma would say.

You think of Ma's bright eyes, determined to the last. *I won't let this place beat me*, you think.

'Well, would you look at this lambkin. A strong wind would blow her away!' says the nearest woman.

'Tsk, her face is a sight, though – enough pox scabs on the lass to frighten the grim reaper,' laughs another. 'We'd give you some oatmeal for your skin, girl – only we ate it all!'

You know you look a sight. You may have survived the smallpox, but your face is still knobbly with sores. You wish you did have some oatmeal to soothe the itchy scabs.

A girl who introduces herself as Annie – a tough, cheeky sort, with a dimple in her chin – shows you the work for the day. You must unwind and pick apart chunks of the old rope. The bosses will then take the rope fluff – oakum – to sell to the

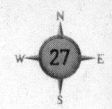

shipyards, where it will be jammed between joints in ships' hulls to stop them from leaking. 'So this old bit of oakum,' laughs Annie, 'will see more of the world than we poor girls ever will!'

At first it seems boring, but easy: just unwind the rope into smaller and smaller threads until you have a fluffy, fibrous mass that reminds you of Da's unruly beard. After three hours, however, it's still boring, but certainly not easy. The tiny, tough rope fibres slice your fingertips. The room is filled with fluff and dust, and the oakum irritates your skin. Your fingernails fill with blood, and blisters pop up on your hands.

By dinnertime, your hands are such a wreck you can't hold a spoon to eat, but instead have to lift the bowl of gruel to your mouth and swallow. Bed is some wooden planks and a rough blanket. The next day is more of the same.

For the first couple of days, it's a shock to wake up and find yourself in the workhouse – but the grim, repetitive days just keep coming, and you soon find yourself retreating into your own faraway thoughts. The life you shared in Kilkenny with Ma, Da and Erin now seems like a distant, pretty dream.

ABOUT A WEEK after your arrival, a lady comes to the poorhouse. A fine lady she is, too, with button-up boots of leather, a crisp skirt that makes a shushing sound as she walks, and a parasol in her hand. She introduces herself as Madam Miriam, and says she runs a school to train young girls to be maids in rich men's houses.

You imagine yourself holding a steaming plate of golden roast potatoes in your hands, serving them to the master's dark wooden table with its gleaming cutlery and starched napkins. All the other girls get stars in their eyes too. You suddenly know that you will give anything on God's green earth to convince Madam Miriam that *you* are the most impeccably mannered, thoughtful, righteous, hard-working and obedient girl in that poorhouse. *You* are going to Madam Miriam's maid school.

In an instant, it all comes true. Madam Miriam chooses you! And so you find yourself whisked out of the poorhouse by the side of this fine, good-smelling lady.

But, as your ma used to say, *If something seems too good to be true, then it probably is.* Down an alleyway, through the back door of a tavern, behind a red velvet curtain you trot, wide-eyed, like a lamb to the slaughter, only realising when you see a man with black teeth and a knife that this is no school for girls.

'This is our thieves' den, pretty girl,' says 'Madam Miriam', unbuttoning her jacket and shaking it off to reveal her tattooed arms. She suddenly switches back to the upper-class accent she used to fool the owner of the poorhouse: 'And you'll join us as a pickpocket from now on, or I'll have your throat slit and your body dumped in the Thames. Isn't that right, Earl?'

The black-toothed man just snickers.

'You're to be the amuser's accomplice,' Madam Miriam continues, 'on account of you looking so sweet and innocent. Earl here, the amuser, will throw snuff into someone's face, to make them cough and sneeze, and then *you* run to their aid, patting them on the back, helping them find their hanky, and helping yourself to their wallet. You bring that wallet right back here to dear Uncle Earl and Aunty Miriam. Then we might get you a lovely roast dinner – can't say fairer than that, now, can we? Unless you'd prefer to dine with the fishes?' she leers.

As the following week passes, and Miriam and Earl train you in how to be a thief – to slip your fingers into coat pockets, lift the contents swiftly, and conceal your pickings – you go over your options again and again in your mind. When your training is finished, you will be set loose

on the streets of London as Earl's apprentice.

It would be a tough, dangerous life, but part of you quite likes the idea of evening the score a little: the poor taking something back from the rich. And if you stick with Miriam and Earl, you might learn a thing or two – and avoid them tossing you in the River Thames as a bonus.

Or you could do a runner. You're fast on your feet, and if you disappeared down a crowded street there'd be a good chance that bony, hunched Earl couldn't keep up with you. From there, you could find yourself an honest job and a place to stay – although you could also find yourself back in the poorhouse.

As the week draws to a close, Miriam announces that she's satisfied with your training, and that tomorrow will be your first day of 'work'. Now's the time to make your decision.

---

* If you choose to become a pickpocket for Miriam and Earl, turn to page 57.
* If you choose to run away from them once you're in a crowded street, turn to page 61.
* To read a fact file on child pickpockets, turn to page 255, then return to this page to make your choice.

You leave your ma with tears in your eyes and a full cup of water by her bedside. The lady's bracelet is secure in the hem of your petticoat, and your winter coat is drawn over your shoulders, though you can feel icy fingers of wind wriggling in through the holes. You drag your heart along the pavement behind you on a string, like some dirty, barely remembered toy.

You work your way up to the high street. Night is falling, but you make your way to the apothecary's lit window, clinging to your last forlorn hope, that with your bracelet you'll buy Ma a cure for smallpox.

The apothecary snorts. 'Do you think little Prince Alfred would have died of smallpox if there were a cure? King Louis of France? Both of King William's parents and his bleeding wife, pardon my language? And a little grub like you asks for a cure? Stop wasting my time and get out of my shop!'

'Please,' you beg him. 'I may look poor, but I can pay. I've got something right here…'

You reach for your petticoat and begin to lift

the hem. He leers at you and you get a sudden, sick feeling in your stomach.

Suddenly you're backing out of the shop as fast as you can go, feeling furious. Of course there's not a cure. But you're sure that wouldn't stop this horrid man from taking your precious bracelet from you. You resolve to keep the bracelet an absolute secret from now on, and never be tricked into parting with it.

It's dark and cold, and you decide you might as well try Mrs Raeburn's for a place to stay, though you don't know her well. When you arrive, however, she takes one look at you and slams the door in your face.

'They say your ma's got the pox,' she shouts through her closed door, 'and I'm not running the risk of having you in this house. I've six children of my own to keep alive!' Then the door opens a crack, and she throws a piece of bread in your direction. 'Take it and go!'

You return home, only to discover that your own door has been locked from the inside. You realise, with a wrench in your heart, that Ma must have used the last of her strength to stagger to the door and lock you out, to protect you from coming back

to look after her. You ball yourself up on your doorstep and cry.

You're not sure how you'll make it through this terrible night, but the dawn does eventually arrive, cold and bright. Mrs Raeburn bustles down the street, hair in a bun, starched work-apron tied to her pudgy body.

'Well, up you get, then,' she says, as if you'd planned to meet her here. 'Come along!' And she nods for you to fall into step behind her.

This woman slammed the door in my face last night, you think. But seeing you huddled in the doorstep of your own home seems to have awakened some sort of bossy maternal instinct in her, as she hustles you along to her workplace at the cloth mill.

'They often need young ones to work here,' she tells you, 'and you may as well have something useful to do, since you don't know what your future holds. You'll be paid twenty pence at the end of each week.' She looks away from you uncomfortably, a mix of pity and annoyance on her face.

These machines spin thread like nothing you've ever seen – a whirling clattering of arms and wheels. The noise of a hundred of them going at once fills the vast room, and the air is hazy with dust and cotton fibres. Cloth spills off the looms in creamy folds, and metal ribs and teeth crunch hungrily.

The job you're given is 'scavenger': you must keep the floor underneath the machines free from dust and fibres, so that nothing gets caught in the machines and jams the mechanism. You have no idea how these machines work, but you can see straight away that if you let your hair or fingers become caught in them, the machines would rip them clean off your body.

Stifling your coughs, you work on your knees for six hours until midday, when you are given a bowl of watery soup. Then you go back to work under the thrashing, pounding machines for another six hours, driven on despite your exhaustion, as you've been told the fierce factory owner won't hesitate to beat anyone who stops to rest.

You're so busy being careful not to fall into one of the machines that you hardly manage to think about Ma all day. By its end, you are so bone-tired that it's only as you're walking down your street, that you remember you're still locked out of your home.

Then you stop. The door is wide open – splintered and busted off its hinges – and there's a horse-and-cart out the front. Two men wearing black, with rags tied over their faces, are lifting something long, covered in a blanket, onto the back of their cart.

'Ma!' you cry, running towards them. But the nearest man puts out his arm. 'She's gone,' he says, his voice muffled beneath the rag. 'Best not to look.'

Your stomach heaves as you glance into the empty house. 'Where are you taking her?' you ask.

'London Cemetery,' comes the muffled reply. 'Pauper's grave.'

You feel a black crow fly in and land heavily on the branches of your heart. An unmarked pauper's grave. You've heard that gravediggers stack the bodies one on top of another at the cemetery, with only a few inches of soil to cover them. The stench can drift for miles on a bad day. Old, rotting bodies are chopped into pieces to make way for the new, and the coffins are sold as firewood. You've even heard of bodies being stolen from graves and sold to medical schools for dissection.

You can't allow Ma to be dumped into the cold earth like that, without even a marker or a prayer;

not when you know she might be dug up again, her bones disturbed and scattered.

You worry that if you don't give Ma a good burial, you'll never feel at peace again; that every memory of her will fill you with guilt. Your nan, who believed in these things, bless her soul, would say it would turn Ma into a ghost, forcing her to roam the earth forever, pleading for release and tormenting those left behind.

You think of the bracelet in the hem of your petticoat. That would certainly be enough to pay for a proper funeral and headstone; to lay Ma to rest the right way. You're just about to offer the bracelet to the stretcher-bearer when you hear your ma's voice in your mind. *Keep your jewels for the living, darling – don't spend them on the dead!*

But then you hear your da's voice saying, *Be good to your ma while I'm gone* – his last words before the soldiers hauled him away to a prison ship on the Thames. And with him locked up, and your sister gone, if you don't honour and remember your ma, who will?

You have almost nothing left in this world, and you know that children like you can live or die from one day to the next as easily as rats. *Except*, you

think, *rats don't have to plan for their future, or honour their dead.*

✦ To offer the stretcher-bearer your bracelet in exchange for a decent burial for Ma, go to page 43.
✦ To keep your bracelet, go to page 38.
✦ To read a fact file about child labour, go to page 257, then return to this page to make your choice.

'Sorry, Ma,' you whisper to yourself, 'but I think I need the bracelet more than you do, right now.'

One day, somehow, you resolve you'll be rich enough to buy roses for every unmarked grave in London.

The stretcher-bearers shuffle off, leaving you alone – so alone. Not a soul in the world knows where you are, and not a soul cares.

No, that's not true – *Da cares*, you think. *And someday, somehow, I'll find him again.*

Since the door to your home is open, you go inside and fossick for any useful possessions, knowing that the landlord will arrive soon to move the next family in. There's not much here that means anything to you anymore, though. You gather up a blanket and a pot, hoping to use, sell or trade them later.

You walk back out into the cobbled street, weighing up your options. You know you must be careful: stray children like yourself are gathered up by constables and dumped in poorhouses to work like slaves. That would be even worse than scavenging for work at the cloth mill as you did today.

Your mind is numb with shock and grief. You're trying to put together a plan to find your da, but you're shifting pieces of ideas around in your mind like a broken puzzle – bracelet; sleep; work; travel; hide – and nothing seems to fit. The light from a nearby tavern draws you in like a moth. Hungry and tired as you are, the beefy smell of an Irish stew is impossible to resist.

No sooner do you step through the doorway than you are yanked into the arms of a man who smells like beer and has one crooked eye that veers off to the left.

'Eat up!' he shouts. 'No one goes hungry when Bobby's won at the races!'

The men in the tavern all shout, 'Hurrah!' The one or two women there, who have loose hair and looser blouses, roll their eyes and laugh. A man plonks a plate of stew down in front of you.

Don't look a gift-horse in the mouth, Ma would have said, and you gobble it up thankfully.

Someone is playing a rollicking jig on a fiddle. The man with the crooked eye is whirling elbow-in-elbow with a tousled brunette, her petticoats flying. The warmth and the heat and the noise seems to be chasing some of the numbness out of you, and you surprise yourself by laughing when a man with a goatee beard and a golden tooth drapes you in a pearl necklace and hoists you onto his shoulders, shouting out, 'Here comes the Queen of all the Irish in London Town!'

A gust of cold wind blows through the tavern as its door is thrown open, and suddenly some of the shouts sound alarmed. The music skids to a halt. People scatter everywhere – out doors, upstairs, under tables – as the sound of whistles and boots fills the room. You are thrown off your perch on the man's shoulders, to the ground.

'They're after Bobby!' you hear someone shout.

One of the women scoffs, 'Won on the races – like hell! I might've known!'

You realise that the pearl necklace the golden-toothed man draped over you is probably stolen, and the room is swarming with constables, so you fling it away as you dash out the back door.

Your bare feet are freezing and your heart is pounding like a drum as you dash down the alleyway. You suddenly remember you've left your pot and blanket inside. As you glance behind you, you hear a snarl, and a dog leaps from a doorway, snapping at your bare legs. You leap away from it

with a scream, stumbling out into the road, right into the path of a horse.

You feel your head bounce as it hits the cobblestones. The hooves and carriage-wheels rain down on you, and your body is pummelled into the ground. You fight to get out from under the cart, but suddenly something in your chest goes *crack*, and you can fight no more. You can't force any air into your lungs. Your mind shouts at your limbs to move, but you can't get up.

'Pfff,' says a voice. 'The carts don't even stop when they knock them down these days. The families breed like rabbits in the slums, and more than half of them end up dead or turned into criminals. Can you hear me, girl?'

You feel a foot prod you. You fight to make a sound, but there is no more air coming in or out of you. Your body is a broken puppet. You feel a strange floating sensation: now you're looking down on your body from above. It's lying in the gutter, and a pair of constables are looking down on it.

Your body is all wrong angles, black with mud and red with blood. Your face looks waxy and empty, like a mask. You feel a stab of pity for the poor, used body, but it isn't yours anymore... you are leaving it behind.

One of the constables is dragging your body out of the gutter. 'This girl's not getting up now, Jim. Probably has a broken neck – she was mighty battered when that horse ran her over. Oh, now here's something...' He has felt the bracelet in your petticoat's hem. 'Seems she has some stolen jewellery on her, too.'

It's not stolen! you want to shout. *It's mine! I need it!* But as you think the words, the need and the anger drop away from you. Your mind is washed clean of its memories and desires. You are rising up through a dark tunnel, and a warm light is thrown down upon you. It's even more beautiful and inviting than the tavern door.

You feel like a child running into your mother's arms – you are rushing upwards towards the light like a twig in a flood. Then you are inside the light, and the light is inside you, and you are everywhere and nowhere all at once. You remember this feeling of boundless peace: you were here before your life began, and now you have returned here... after your life has ended.

THE END

✦ To return to your last choice and try again, go to page 37.

You snap the row of stitches along your hem, fish out the precious bracelet, and show it to the stretcher-bearer.

'Will this be enough to get my ma a decent funeral?' you ask.

He puts your ma's body down gently on the cart and steps towards you, leaving the second man behind with the cart. He tugs the rag away from his face, and you see now that his face is kind and gentle, though ravaged by smallpox scars.

He's lucky to still be alive, you think.

'Now, what did a wee lass like you do to come by a treasure like that?' he asks warmly.

'I saved a lady from a horse. It was panicked 'cos her carriage broke,' you whisper. 'Happened just yesterday.'

You can see from the way he nods earnestly that he believes you. 'Do you have any family left?' he asks you huskily.

You shake your head.

'I know what it feels like,' he tells you. 'Sometimes I wish it'd been me who was taken instead. I had

the pox and survived, but my little daughter didn't. She would have been about your age, had she lived. Claire, her name was.'

He heaves a sigh. Then his large, bear-like hand reaches out and wraps over yours, folding the bracelet into your palm.

'You keep this,' he says. 'And don't tell anyone else you have it. I know another way to get your ma a decent burial.'

He introduces himself as Mr MacIntosh, and invites you to his home, to meet his wife and have some tea by the fire. Mrs MacIntosh turns out to be as humble and warm-hearted as her husband. Their surviving children have all grown up and left home.

They explain that Mrs MacIntosh works as a cook in a mansion on the outskirts of London, which is in need of a girl to help cook, clean, chop kindling and feed the animals. You can hardly believe your luck, especially when you learn that there is a stable too, with six fine horses in it.

You agree to give your first month's pay to the MacIntoshes, to pay for a simple but respectable burial for your ma. They have room for you to stay the night, and clean clothes for you to put on before you start work at the mansion in the morning. You sew your bracelet back inside your petticoat hem, as

that seems as secure a place as you can think of for now, and you feel very grateful to have met such a kind couple.

The next morning you discover that the lord of the mansion, however, is anything but kind-hearted. He looks you up and down with distaste, his upper lip sneering under his wiry moustache.

'Couldn't you find anything better?' he asks Mrs MacIntosh, as if she had gone to the butcher's for roast beef and come back with a chicken bone. 'Very well, then – but mind she doesn't get under my feet, or I will throw her back onto the scrap heap from whence she undoubtedly came.'

He agrees to give you a few hours away from your duties later that week to travel with Mr MacIntosh to a garden cemetery, where your ma is buried in the shade of an elm tree with a simple tombstone. There's no money for a priest, but Mr MacIntosh recites a Bible verse, and you sing an Irish song. Ma can rest in peace now. You've done the right thing.

Back at work, you've made friends with Elsie, the serving-girl, who is gossipy and good fun, and only a few years older than you.

'The master used to have a missus,' she whispers eagerly over the potato peelings one day, 'and they say she drowned, but you know what I reckon? He *killed* her!' She continues breathlessly, 'I was in the dining room one day, setting out the lunch, and suddenly I *feel* him there – you know, like ice on my spine! And I turn around to see him standing there, staring – just staring, right at me – with a *knife* in his hand!'

'Oh, hush, girls,' butts in Mrs MacIntosh. 'Less tongue-wagging and more work, now!'

Elsie shoots you a conspiratorial wink.

The days pass, and Elsie always saves you the best leftover roast potatoes and cream cake from the master's meals. One day, she shows you something twinkly and tiny nestled in her hand: a pair of cufflinks she has stolen from the master's dressing-room.

'What do you say?' she asks. 'Want to go into business with me?'

Elsie's boyfriend Jack, you learn, has agreed to come to the back gate and spirit away any small, worthwhile items she can procure, to sell at the market for a good price.

'Jack's taking all the risk, really,' says Elsie admiringly.

You're not sure that's true – she's the one stealing things from under the master's nose. Elsie wants you to carry the treasures down to the chicken pen

at the bottom of the garden for her, as it's your job to empty the vegetable peelings there.

'Toss the trinkets over the back fence by the chicken pen, and Jack will pick them up,' she says. Your face must look doubtful, because she goes on: 'If anyone finds something in the bucket, just say you've no idea how it got there! Oh, come on – the master's a murderous old sod, and he has more of these little baubles than he can count! I'll give you a quarter of every pound we earn.'

Your heart races. If you said yes, you'd be rich in no time. Your part in the scheme would only be a small one, really... and soon you could travel along the Thames to find Da's prison ship, and bribe a gaoler to let you see him.

But, you tell yourself, Mrs MacIntosh expects better of you... and stealing is wrong – although perhaps not quite as wrong as the fact that nasty, selfish people like the master are dripping with gold while poor people like yourself have none.

'Will you do it?' asks Elsie, her face alight.

✦ To help Elsie with her thieving scheme, go to page 53.

✦ If you refuse to help Elsie steal, go to page 48.

Elsie's face turns stone-cold when you tell her you don't want to partake in her thieving scheme. For a moment, there is a narrowness to her eyes that scares you, and you wonder if you've made an enemy. But then her face brightens, and she laughs and points at you.

'Ha, tricked you! I'd never steal from the master – do you think I'm daft? I just wanted to see if *you* would.' She chuckles as she walks away.

All right then, Elsie, you think as you watch her go. *But what are you going to do with that pair of cufflinks I just saw you slip back into your pocket?*

You don't rat on Elsie – you feel a sense of solidarity with her and the other workers in the mansion, and besides, she's still your friend. But from that point on, there is a definite cooling-off in her attitude towards you.

A few days later, you overhear Marion, the senior maid, tell Elsie she needs an extra pair of hands to help serve guests at the luncheon, and ask if you'd

be a good choice. This would be a significant rise in your household status.

But Elsie replies loftily, 'Oh, Marion, I wouldn't trust *that* little child to carry a boiled egg and toast! Have you seen how careless she is in the kitchen? She drives poor Mrs MacIntosh half mad!'

Your ears burn. You're not careless! You keep your conversations with Elsie to a minimum after that.

You've been at the mansion for two weeks, and are slowly repaying your debt to the MacIntoshes. One gusty winter's day, you pop outside to empty the scraps. You stop by the stables, as you do nearly every day, to give the horses some apple cores. You love their snuffly hot noses nudging your hand, their gentle snorts, and their shining brown eyes.

'Fancy I could let you ride one, if you're keen,' says Jeremy, the stableboy.

'Really?' you gasp.

'Sure. They like you well enough.' He shrugs. 'What with all the treats you give them! I'd start you out on Minty; she's a gentle old soul.'

You can hardly believe it! You are almost skipping back to the house when you hear wails and sobbing drifting from an upstairs window.

'I'd *never* do something like that, master!' squeals Elsie's voice. 'Honest to God, I'd sooner die!'

Uh-oh, you think, and your heart starts to race.

Elsie goes on: 'Forgive me for speaking plainly, master, but you say this has been going on for a few weeks – and only *one* of us arrived in your service a few weeks ago. I know she's naught but a little girl, but still, she's shifty, and if you check her belongings, I'd wager you'll find some of the items you're missing…'

You rush to the kitchen and frantically start going through your belongings. Because suddenly you don't trust Elsie further than you could kick her, and any moment now the master is going to—

Slam! The master is upon you like a wave of fury, his grey moustache seeming as though it could shoot sparks. He has you by the collar, and he's snarling and baring his teeth like an organ-grinder's monkey. 'Where are they?' he spits. 'My wife's earrings? Out with it!'

'I don't know what you mean, sir,' you stammer.

But he twists the neck of your clothes tighter and shouts: 'You were rifling through your belongings just then – trying to hide something!'

You only have one treasure you know of: your

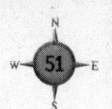

bracelet, sewn into the hem of your petticoat. How on earth will you explain that, let alone be allowed to keep it?

Elsie has followed the master downstairs. Her eyes are very bright. 'Perhaps you should check the hem of her apron, sir?' she suggests quietly. 'I've heard thieves sometimes sew valuables in there.'

Your heart stops. The hem of your *apron*?

The master grabs the garment's lower hem, without bothering to untie it from your waist first, and runs his fingers along it. Suddenly he gasps.

'Yes!' he cries. 'What have we here?'

He grabs a knife from the kitchen table, and you recoil as he plunges it towards your leg – but instead of stabbing you, he slits open the hem of your apron, and out roll two sapphire earrings and a pair of familiar cufflinks: the very ones Elsie showed you when she asked you to join her thieving scheme.

You can't believe what's happening. Your first crushing disappointment is the thought that Jeremy will now never have the chance to teach you to ride Minty. Your second is seeing Mrs MacIntosh shake her head sorrowfully as the master forcibly ejects you and your few worldly belongings from the house – your debt to her and her kind husband

will never be repaid. The third and final blow is the constable who arrives to take you away, saying smugly, 'Well, missy, you'll most likely hang for this.'

You still have the bracelet in the hem of your petticoat, but it seems unlikely that it can save you now.

✱ In this matter you have no choice. Go to page 65.

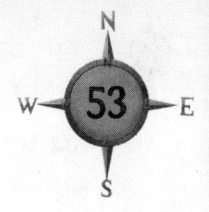

'All right,' you say, feeling a thrill of fear, 'I'll do it.'

Elsie gives a tiny squeal and squeezes your hand. 'We'll start with these cufflinks, then,' she says, dropping them into the scraps bucket beside you.

It's so easy. You merely pop down to the garden to feed the scraps to the chickens as usual, only now there is a grinning, freckled face on the other side of the fence every now and again – that of the brave and daring Jack, who you must admit is rather good fun. You can see why Elsie is attracted to him, even if his ears do stick out.

The scheme works well for the first week – *very* well. You have enough to repay your debt to the MacIntoshes – though you'll give it to them bit by bit, so they don't get suspicious. Between your wages and the money Elsie gives you, you've even saved a little extra money to put towards your planned journey to find Da. The jewelled bracelet is still sewn securely inside your hem, as well.

Sometimes you question whether you're doing

the wrong thing by stealing from the master – but then a little more money will arrive from some sales Jack has made, and you'll squirrel it away, feeling like you're another golden step closer to seeing your da again, and decide that it's worth it.

As the week has progressed, though, Elsie has started to get bolder. One day a pocket watch as large as a biscuit slips out of her sleeve and into the vegetable peelings... and once that's been successfully passed over the fence, the next day it's an ornate drinking goblet so large it hits the side of the scraps bucket with a *clang*. As she hurriedly buries it in potato peelings, Elsie gets the giggles and can't stop – but you are growing ever more apprehensive.

At the end of that second week at the mansion, something amazing happens – Jeremy the stableboy promises to let you ride one of the six gorgeous horses who wait for you every day, hoping for an apple core when you come to visit them and rub their gleaming necks.

You can't think of anything better. 'Won't the master be angry, though?' you ask Jeremy.

'Naw,' he replies. 'It was mostly the missus who rode them, before she passed away, and the master

hasn't the heart to let them go. They need to be ridden regularly or they'll get stiff and ill.'

You've never thought of the master having a heart before now. Your secret guilt about the thefts grows stronger.

Later that day, you finish washing the kitchen pans and turn to see Mrs MacIntosh holding a pair of sapphire earrings in her big, red hand, staring from the earrings to the scraps bucket and back in disbelief. Your heart stops in its tracks.

Elsie comes into the room and takes in the scene. Her face turns the colour of cold porridge.

'The master's coming!' she gasps. She glances wildly around the room, like a trapped animal, and then, to your utter horror, she whips two silk hankies from under her apron and thrusts them down the neck of your shirt, hissing, 'He mustn't find these on me!'

Mrs MacIntosh drops the earrings back into the scraps bucket like they are burning coals.

As the master steps into the room, he sees you trying to throttle Elsie with one hand, pulling his dead wife's handkerchiefs out of your shirt with the other. And you know, then and there, that there's no excuse in the world that will save you now.

You are right. Jack gets away scot-free. Elsie lies, sacrificing you to save herself, ashen-faced. Mrs MacIntosh sadly shakes her head and remains silent as the master shouts furiously at you. Jeremy is sent to find a constable to come and take you away.

You realise, too late, that perhaps the master did have a heart, for he only paid any attention to the things he had lost when Elsie started to steal his wife's jewellery and hankies. His own things, it seems, meant nothing to him, but every possession of his dead wife's was a treasure... including the six fine horses down in the stables, which you will now never ride.

✳ In this matter you have no choice. Go to page 65.

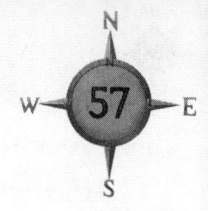

Today is the first day of your new life as a pickpocket – Earl's apprentice. Miriam scrubbed you down with hot water and brushed your hair last night, and now you are wearing a forget-me-not-blue dress, lovely red coat and real leather shoes. The reflection that greeted you in the mirror this morning was that of a well-loved, privileged child. If only that were true.

The marketplace is bustling. You see the barrow-lady with her roses and carnations, hear shouts and wet slaps from the fishmonger's stall, and smell pipe-tobacco and freshly baked bread.

You watch Earl out of the corner of your eye. He is weaving his way through the crowd, oily and unnoticed, scanning people up and down, searching for a suitable target – someone rich, unaccompanied, and not particularly strong.

In Earl's hand is a little tin of snuff – a fine, light-brown powder made from tobacco leaves. People snort it directly into their noses rather than burning it in a pipe. Earl let you smell a pinch of it during

your training, and it felt like weevils were clawing their way up your nostrils. You sneezed violently for a good half-hour afterwards. You don't envy the person who's about to have a whole tin of it thrown in their face.

A fleeting smile twists the corner of Earl's mouth. He moves purposefully towards a lady with a wicker basket hanging over one arm, who is inspecting a barrow of oranges. You duck in a wide arc through the crowd, to get to the other side of the barrow, ready to be in a perfect position to 'assist' the lady when Earl strikes. She has pink, fat cheeks and pearl buttons on her blouse.

It's all right, ma'am, you think to yourself. *Earl and I aren't going to hurt you – just make your pockets a little lighter.*

Your hands are sweating. You mentally run through what Miriam told you: *Your right hand's to distract them – brush the snuff away, pat their back, offer a hanky. Your left hand's to do the work – first check their bags; then their outside pockets, left and right; and finally their coat's inner pocket. And you'll talk all the while. Don't stop talking.*

Earl opens his tin as if to pinch some snuff for himself, then trips theatrically. He showers the lady in snuff, and manages to knock over the orange barrow for good measure.

You are stumbling through the rolling oranges, trying to get to the shrieking lady. Already Earl has vanished. The lady is coughing and retching, sneezing and gasping, flailing around like a swarm of bees is after her.

You hurry to her side, but she swats at you as you try to offer your help. In the end, you have to shout to offer your assistance: *'Let me help you, ma'am!'* She doesn't seem at all grateful.

'Wretched sod – catch him!' she shouts.

You think maybe Earl underestimated this lady. In all the scenarios you've practised, the 'victim' (Earl or Miriam) would gratefully and docilely accept your assistance. This is not going at all to plan.

You persevere, brushing at the snuff on the lady's jacket – but real snuff was never used when you practised, so when you accidentally breathe in a cloud of it, you are absolutely unprepared. You explode into a volley of violent sneezes.

Part of you wants to give up and get out of here now, even if it will earn you a beating from Miriam. But you stubbornly and clumsily persist, your right hand offering a hanky while your left hand digs

around in the lady's basket until it feels the metal clasp of a coin-purse. Success!

As you lift the purse from the basket, you hear the fruit-seller shout, 'Oi!' and point a finger at you. You run, trying to disappear swiftly into the crowd like Earl did, but the fruit-seller is fast and strong. Moments later, he has you by the arm, and you're done for.

You wriggle futilely as he says to the lady, 'There are all kinds of scum pulling tricks on the streets of London these days, ma'am. But don't worry – this one won't get away with it. *Constable!*'

✢ In this matter you have no choice. Go to page 65.

You pretend to go along with Miriam and Earl's plans, but secretly, you are planning to dash off as soon as you have the chance. You will run all day and night if need be, and the next and the next, until you find your da's prison ship. You just want to talk to him, to see his face, and to give him your word that you haven't forgotten him.

Of course, you think, *he won't know about Ma yet. I'll have to tell him.* Your heart sinks.

You are in the thieves' den. Miriam is forcefully brushing your hair, trying to tame you into a picture of innocence – a well-bred child no one would suspect of pickpocketing, ready for your first day of work for her. Your face is cleaner than it has been in weeks, and you're wearing a sky-blue dress, a lovely red coat, and real leather shoes that Miriam has managed to snaffle from somewhere. You imagine your da's proud, astonished face when you greet him wearing this perfect outfit.

Your jewelled bracelet is still in your petticoat

hem. You're so glad you've managed to keep it hidden from Miriam.

You pray Earl isn't fast on his feet. You don't expect he will be, as he's so bony and hunched. You don't have to worry about Miriam chasing you – she's told you she'll stay here, awaiting your return with riches for her.

When the time comes to leave, Earl walks closely beside you until you reach the edge of a bustling marketplace.

'I'll take a while to choose the right one,' he hisses in your ear. 'Some nice easy pickings for starters. Watch me, and stay nearby, but not so near as anyone'd spot we're together. You have to be first on the scene to help once I've thrown the snuff. Got it?'

You nod, your heart pounding. The market is a scene of happy, industrious chaos: newspaper-boys shouting the day's news; peddlers with pushcarts selling everything from candles to rat poison; stalls piled high with turnips and greens.

Earl slips away through the crowd, like a hot knife through butter. You are surprised at how agile he suddenly seems. You want to wait till he's a good distance away before you run, so you don't move, letting him get further and further away... but he

shoots you an annoyed glance. He's noticed you're not following him!

You begin to move towards him, but the next time he turns away, you duck behind a stall selling yards of cloth.

You take a deep breath, and then run like the wind. Your new leather shoes pinch at your feet. You don't dare look behind you for Earl; you only pray you had enough of a head start and that he's lost you.

You make for the edge of the marketplace, ducking around baskets and squeezing between people like a mouse in a kitchen. You feel as though you might just make it... not far now!

You squeal as someone catches your arm in a vice-like grip. Fingernails dig into you, and you look up to see Miriam's face, tight-lipped with fury, her eyes gleaming in triumph.

'I thought you might try something like this,' she hisses. A couple of people turn to stare. 'Darling!' she exclaims abruptly, in a voice as sweet as toffee. 'Mummy was so worried! Come along now!'

She yanks you out of the marketplace, despite your best efforts to kick her in the shins.

Back at the thieves' den, Earl wheedles: 'What

say *I* go to the poorhouse this time, Miriam? I can pick them better! You always bring back feisty ones who run off.'

'Shut up,' snarls Miriam. She yanks the rope she's tied around your wrists even tighter.

'I'll be good!' you squeal. 'I won't run away again! Give me another chance!'

'If chances were pennies, lass, then you'd be dead broke,' chuckles Earl. 'Though as it is...I guess you'll just be dead.'

Earl pulls a hessian sack over your head. You fight to breathe.

The last thing you hear is his voice: 'Oh well, there are always more girls wanting to go to Madam Miriam's Maid School.'

Then Miriam knocks you over the head with a frying pan, and everything goes black.

THE END

✳ To return to your last choice and try again, go to page 30.

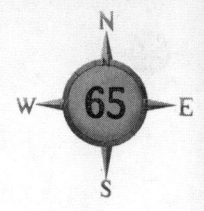

The sky is grey and the wind is biting. Your hands are cuffed in front of you with heavy chains. The constable prods you roughly in your back with his truncheon every few paces, making you stumble as you approach Newgate Prison on shaking legs.

You turn a corner and see the front wall of the gaol, a towering edifice of bluestone. There is an enormous wooden platform erected outside the front gate – the gallows. An empty noose swings from its frame. A knot of nausea tightens in your stomach, and you keep your face turned away from the gallows as you pass. When you first came to London, you and Ma heard cheering and, thinking it was a carnival and hoping to see travelling performers, you followed the noise to the front of the gaol – just as a condemned man dropped to his death. You both looked away in horror, but too late. You can't ever forget that sight. *Is that what will happen to me too?* you wonder. You try to shove the thought out of your mind.

Though the light from the wintry sky is weak, you shiver as you come under the shadow cast by the forbidding bulk of Newgate Prison. The bluestone walls seem designed to block out any glimmer of light, or hope of escape. You shudder as the gates creak open. You don't know how long you will be locked in here before you are sentenced and learn your fate: it could be months, or years. All you know is that inside the gaol is the stuff of nightmares: rats that nibble your ears and fingertips off while you sleep; sicknesses that can strike a hundred prisoners dead in a week; lice that infest your hair, clothes and skin. Newgate Prison is a deep, black pit, seething with violent criminals. No candle to light your way. No parents to protect you.

Standing in the iron gateway, you baulk like a nervy horse. Your legs have stopped working: you know you have to take the next step inside the gaol, but you can't do it. Goodbye, sky. Goodbye, fresh air. Goodbye to being able to run, or climb a tree, or jump a stream. Your knees are knocking.

The constable has seen this before: he swings his truncheon hard against the tendons at the back of your knees, making your legs buckle forward, and you stumble inside the gaol. As the gates clang closed behind you, your heart begins to pound so violently that you feel you might be sick.

Tears leak from your eyes, but you clench your teeth fiercely. You manage to raise your chained hands to your face to wipe the tears away. To be seen crying in front of the other prisoners would mark you out as a weakling. You will have to be tougher than old boots to get by in here – and fierce and vigilant to stop the precious bracelet in your hem being discovered, and stolen from you. You're certain there will be people in here, both prisoners and wardens, who'd happily murder you for half as much.

A warden unlocks your handcuffs and hustles you forward down a corridor, deeper inside the gaol. The stench that fills this place – a putrid odour of sewage and rotting filth – is so vile that it feels like a living thing, forcing itself into your nostrils and down your throat. You breathe carefully through your mouth, trying not to gag or pass out.

The cell you are thrown into is dank and subterranean, about the size of a barn but with a low ceiling. It's crowded with about fifty ragged women and a few children. Mercifully, it has an opening in one of its slimy, black stone walls – a window lined with iron bars, at head height. The window lets in

a little light and air, and through it you can see the feet and ankles of those walking by directly outside at street level. Some of the prisoners glance at you when you arrive: a few with glazed, indifferent eyes; others with faces prickly with hostility. You shrink back against a wall, not saying anything – just waiting and watching, until you can learn if there's anyone here to trust.

A few of the women crowd under the little window, extending their hands and calling out pleadingly to passers-by. You watch them do this for hours, wondering why they bother to keep at it – until, just before dusk, a passer-by throws the tail end of a loaf of bread down through the hole. A broad, blonde woman catches it, then fights off the others with one hand as she shoves the food into her mouth with the other, chewing and swallowing as fast as she can, even as her hair's being yanked by one of the others.

As darkness falls, the prison guard drops a single scoop of watery slop into a bowl for you. You eat it quickly, but there's still a gnawing hole in your belly. *So that's how you get by in here*, you think. *Those who are tough enough to stand at the window the longest, and fight the hardest, get something extra.*

I can do that, you think, a little flame of hope lighting inside you. *And I'll be lucky tomorrow – I know I will.*

ANKLES. ALL THE next morning, you watch ankles and feet passing by the window. Your eyes follow them as keenly as a dog on a scent: leather shoes, some broad and black, some dainty and tan, plodding and tapping. When you stand right under the window and look up, you can see people's faces, too.

'Milady!' you shout as a parasol swings by.

'Please, sir!' you call to a man in black who's stopped to check his watch.

Plenty of them look wealthy enough to spare you a coin or a crust, but none of them do.

Hours pass, and your arms ache from holding them up to the window. You can see why most of the prisoners don't bother with this: it's disheartening and exhausting. But just then, a middle-aged man in a cap and brown waistcoat passes by.

'Here you go, love,' he says kindly, and he tosses something down to you that flashes in midair and hits the stone rim of the window with a clink.

You snatch up the coin from the floor where it falls. Then you dart away and hold it tightly in your hand as the other women who were also at the window grab at you and yell.

'Oi, you've only been here one day. Give it to me!' shouts one, pummelling you. You manage to elbow her in the face, and she screams. She raises a hand to strike you when a shout from one of the other prisoners makes everyone run back to the window.

'Men prisoners! They're bringing a load in for sentencing!'

It's hard to see past the crowd that's formed under the window. 'What's going on?' you ask a brown-haired girl standing beside you.

'They've brought some men in from one of the other prisons, or the hulks maybe, to be taken to the Old Bailey next door for sentencing,' she explains.

You plunge into the crowd and wriggle your way to the front to get a better look. A line of men comes up the street, being herded like tired sheep by guards with truncheons at the ready. Iron shackles on their wrists and ankles are linked to a long chain that clinks as they shuffle along. The women who are crowded around you at the window jostle to see the men better, and some of them cheer.

As you watch the line trudge past, your eyes scanning each exhausted, unfamiliar face with pity, suddenly a figure catches your eye – a tall, broad man with a ginger beard. Your heart stops. It's him!

'Da!' you scream at the top of your voice. His head swings around, looking for the sound. 'Da, down here! Da! *Da!*'

He sees you, and his mouth drops open in astonishment. He can barely walk in those chains, let alone break free, but he's wrenching at them and lurching about with all his bodily strength anyway. He is trying to get closer to you, and he's bending down to look at you better through the bars. The other prisoners chained to him are shouting, and shuffling towards you too, trying to help him get closer. Wardens come running down the street. Inside your cell, the women around you shove and cheer, hoisting you up closer to the hole.

'It's you!' you hear Da shout above the din. 'Oh, dear God, what's happened to you, my love?'

You slip an arm out of the window, but he's too far away to touch. He struggles to reach out to you, but his chains make it impossible. You start to cry.

The last time Da shouted to you like this, his voice full of tears and love, was as they dragged him

away a year ago. Now, again, he is fighting to get back to you – gaunt and pale as a ghost, but his eyes shining like jewels.

'Da!' you manage to cry again through your tears.

'Eyes to the ground!' barks a warden outside, but the prisoners don't comply: everyone is staring at the thirteen-year-old waif at the window with tears coursing down her cheeks, and her convict father struggling to reach her.

'I *said* eyes to the *ground*!' shouts the warden again. He cracks his truncheon into his palm as a warning, and all the men hastily look at their toes – except your da. He can't tear his eyes from yours.

You don't want to tell him about Ma, but he has to know. You manage to choke the words out, half sob, half shout: 'Ma...she's dead! The smallpox took her.'

'You'll be whipped for this!' shouts the warden with the truncheon.

Da has crumpled in half with grief...but then he straightens. 'To hell with you and your chains!' he shouts. 'Stay strong, my darling! I promise I'll find you! I prom—'

The warden starts using his truncheon to pound Da's body like he's tenderising a piece of meat.

Another warden starts moving the chain of men onwards towards the Old Bailey, past your window, dragging Da with them.

You are hiccupping with sobs now, your shoulders shaking. But as Da disappears out of sight, your tears subside. The tiny flicker of hope and determination you felt last night burns brighter and begins to glow in your belly – a fire to warm you all the way through. Da is alive – he is right next door – and you *will* see each other again. You must. To hell with them and their chains.

SLEEP IS IMPOSSIBLE that night. What sentence did Da get? Will he be hanged, or transported? How will he keep his promise to find you again? The stone floor and your thin blanket give you no comfort. Your position beneath the window is the coldest spot in the freezing room – everybody else huddles as far away from it as possible at night, like sheep in bad weather – but you've found you cannot bring yourself to leave that one small opening into the world outside now, not even while you sleep.

In the darkest part of the night, when the noises of Newgate have faded away to an occasional clank

or shout, and when the air coming in through the barred window is black and frigid, a voice cackles in your ear, making you jump.

'I saw the whole thing,' whispers a hoarse voice. 'Little daughter, did what she oughta. Dad was trying, you were crying. Am I right?'

You leap to your feet – and realise the voice is drifting into the cell from outside. You peer up into the window and your eyes slowly make out a figure crouching on the ground outside: a nose, two gleaming eyes in a thatch of wrinkles, a mouth black as a rotting pit, and a haze of pale hair over a scabbed scalp.

'I be Nell,' says this strange creature. 'This be Hell. Now let me tell you, little winklet, what Nelly doesn't know isn't worth knowing. Nell knows the name of every flea that crawls on your body. Nell knows how, and who, to tell. She has ears on the ceiling and eyes up the gaolers' nostrils. Nell knows the shape of every key that turns in every lock. *Tick, tock.*'

You feel a shudder run over you. Nell looks so weathered and diseased that she seems like a creature from a nightmare nightmare – or from one of Granny's old tales about witches who steal babies.

You're about to move away when she reaches a hand through the bars and runs a fingernail down the side of your face. She has power in her fingertips. Your skin rises into goosebumps, and you feel weirdly compelled to ask her something.

'I saw my da outside today. Can you help me find him again? He's a prisoner on a men's hulk, but I'm not sure where exactly. I want to know what sentence he was given today.'

She gives a wheezy laugh. 'Nell can pass messages. Nell moves like smoke through these walls. But there's a cost, to get back what you lost. Nothing here's free but the fleas. You see?'

You think of the golden bracelet, safe inside the hem of your petticoat. No, that's out of the question – you can't give her that. It is your biggest secret in here; if the other prisoners knew you had it, you'd be murdered for it in an instant. Then you remember your twopence – but you're not sure about giving her that either. It's all you have in here right now.

'I...I don't have any money,' you lie, 'but I promise that later, when I get out of here, I...' You falter, and stop. Making promises to Nell suddenly seems unwise.

Nell snorts. 'The promise of a pauper, a scabby little daughter, a pinch of pepper and the rest's all water. Money, coins, treasure – that's how to pay Nelly proper. Your da's the Irish cove with the ginger beard, big bones, bright eyes. You be the bird that sings in his empty heart. Nelly knows.'

You blink, feeling stunned and unsure. Nell is creepy and smells foul – and you're going to need more than just your one thin blanket and a daily bowl of gruel to survive long in this place. But although Nell's mad, she seems to know things. Maybe she earns her living by running favours for prisoners. You almost believe that she *could* bring back a message from your da. Knowing his sentence – especially if it's transportation, not hanging – could give you the courage you need to survive this place. But is it worth paying Nell to find out?

✦ To keep your twopence and steer clear of Nell, go to page 77.

✦ To give Nell the twopence in the hope she'll find Da and tell you his sentence, go to page 84.

✦ To read more about prisons, go to page 259, then return to this page to make your choice.

You decide to be practical, and keep your coin. You're sure to need it, and it would be risky to trust somebody as strange as Nell.

'Sorry, Nell,' you say, turning away from the window. 'I don't have any money.'

Nell makes a noise like a spitting cat and melts into the night. Perhaps she will simply go on to the next window now and try to convince somebody else to give up their money.

Following another full day standing by the window hoping for more coins – with no success – you decide that enough is enough: you are freezing cold, and it's foolish to sleep by the window in this weather. You will sleep on the far side of the cell tonight, like the others. As you move towards the dark edges of the room, hoping to find a corner to sleep in, your foot connects with something soft, and you stumble and fall backwards onto a blanket.

There's a screech. The blanket lurches under you – apparently you have fallen down on top of someone. You hastily stand up, but it's too late – a ferocious-

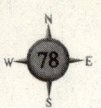

looking woman throws you off her so forcefully that you land on the stone floor with a thud, and she leaps to her feet. She has a horsey face with wide nostrils, and thick hair in a bun.

'Little wench!' she snorts. 'How dare you sit your bony cheeks down on top of me!'

Your heart is pounding, but you can hear your ma's words in your mind: *Never let yourself be bullied, my dear. Nobody will respect you if you let them walk all over you.*

You get to your feet and find your voice. 'I'd rather have bony cheeks than a bony heart.'

The woman's eyes flare. Chuckles and 'ooh's bubble in the crowd that has gathered around you.

'You little...grub! Are you insulting me?'

Your palms are sweaty, but you're not ready to back down. 'Oh no, ma'am,' you say. 'My ma always taught me to be kind to simpletons.'

Hoots of laughter erupt from the crowd. Heat is pumping through your veins. The horsey-faced woman looks like she doesn't know what to say. Then, to your amazement, she also begins snorting with laughter. She gives you a playful clip over the ear.

'I'd never have picked a little scrap like you as a survivor,' she says, chuckling. 'But perhaps you are, lass. Perhaps you are.'

She sits back down on her blanket, and you move away to another corner of the cell, feeling quietly proud of yourself.

A girl not much older than you claps you on the back. 'That was incredible!' she says delightedly. 'Ellen's been here forever – and she rules the roost. I've never seen anyone stand up to her!'

You recognise her as the brown-haired girl who explained what was happening yesterday, when Da and his group of prisoners were being taken to the courthouse. She has friendly brown eyes, a round face, and a thick, matted brown plait hanging over one shoulder.

'I'm Sarah,' she says. 'That was your da who went past yesterday, wasn't it? Do you know what sentence he was given?'

You smile and shrug. Then your smile fades. 'He burnt a government ship – it was a protest for Irish freedom. He's waited a year already for sentencing. Do you think he'll hang?'

The girl considers you seriously, biting her lip. 'They'll give him a heavy penalty, no doubt. But I'd wager he'll get transported – perhaps for life. Plenty of us in here did worse than him and have escaped the noose.'

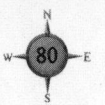

You nod gratefully, overwhelmed by emotion. If Da doesn't hang, then a smaller crime such as yours isn't likely to be punished by death either. Perhaps you will both survive. You manage to give Sarah a little smile. 'How long have you been in here?' you ask her.

'A few months,' Sarah replies. 'I've been sentenced to transportation. Most of us here in this cell are bound for the colonies eventually. I hope we'll sail soon. Maybe you and I will be on the same boat.'

'I'd like that,' you say. 'If I get sentenced to transportation, and so does my da, do you think it's possible he and I will end up in the same colony?'

It's almost too much to hope for – that you and Da might both escape hanging, and be sent to the same land, at the end of the earth.

Sarah smiles wistfully. 'Well, it's always possible, but you'd need the luck of the gods on your side,' she replies. 'There are many colonies in far-flung places, and any of us might end up waiting for years in gaol before we're transported. Still, no one can stop you from hoping. Just behave yourself, for I'm afraid they don't take kindly to rebels in here.'

WEEKS PASS. SARAH shows you how to survive in the rough, filthy world of Newgate: which guards to avoid at all cost, and how waiting at the end of the food line sometimes means you get the thicker, more substantial stew at the bottom of the pot. She also introduces you to a prisoner who knows how to read and write and who says she can write a letter to Da for you for fourpence. You keep a tight hold of your twopence and pray for another one, but without success.

One morning, you wake from weird dreams about a gaolor cutting off your fingers to sell as sausages for a bonfire to discover that your shiny bronze twopence is gone from its hiding spot beneath your blanket. You hurriedly search the folds of your clothes and the cracks of the stones where you slept, but it's really gone. Somebody must have pinched it from under your sleeping body in the night.

You look around and see Ellen, the big, horsey-faced brute, slumped in a corner, watching you. Her head is lolling to one side, and an idiot's drooling smile is spread across her mouth.

'Missing something, pet?' she slurs.

You see the cup in her hand, and stride across the

room as, around you, the other women and their children stir and wake. Sure enough, Ellen's cup is filled with a brown, reeking liquid – alcohol, which she must have bought from a gaolor in the middle of the night after she stole your twopence.

So this is how she's going to punish me for standing up to her, you think. *She might think I'm a survivor, but she still wants to be sure I know my place.*

You're frustrated, but more than anything you just feel sorry for Ellen. She was born right here in Newgate, and has known precious little kindness in her life. The few times she's been let out, she's immediately reoffended and been sent back – the fist of Newgate has squeezed her into a shape that only feels at home in a cell. Ellen doesn't know how to live as a free woman.

Sarah is at your side. She shakes her head, with sadness in her eyes.

'That was my twopence,' you mutter angrily.

Sarah links her arm in yours. 'Bloody drink,' she sighs, and there's a bitterness to her voice you haven't heard before. 'It took more than just twopence from me. I'd be free right now if it weren't for that evil stuff.'

'Did you used to drink, Sarah?' you ask, feeling a little scared of the demons of your friend's past.

'No, never,' she says immediately. 'It was Da...'

Then she trails off into silence.

Sensing she's about to clam up, you put your arm around her shoulders. 'It's all right,' you say. 'You can tell me what happened. Go on...'

✦ To continue with the story, go to page 103.

'All right,' you say. Nell's eyes light up greedily, and you feel a rumbling of unease, but you press on, passing the twopence up through the bars of the window and into Nell's claw-like fingers. It glistens in the moonlight.

'Send a message to my da. Tell him...'

You want to say, *Tell him I love him*, but you need to think of something more useful than that.

'Tell him I'm awaiting sentencing, and hoping for transportation. Tell him I'll keep watch for him every day from this window, just in case. And find out his sentence – promise me, Nell. I have to know what happened,' you urge her.

Nell chuckles. 'Leave it with Nelly, little birdie. Best deal you've made yet, now don't forget.'

Then she melts away into the night. You wonder if you'll ever see her again.

You feel a hand on your arm, and spin to see a round-faced girl not much older than you, with concerned brown eyes and a thick plait. You recognise her as the girl who explained what was happening when Da was taken past the window.

'Did you just agree to give Nell money?' she whispers.

You nod sheepishly.

She shakes her head and rolls her eyes. 'She's always hanging around the streets here. I think she's mad as a hatter. Mind you, some do say she has... well... *powers*. Witchcraft and the like,' she adds, dropping her voice to an even lower whisper.

You shudder. A few months ago, when you had a home and a ma and you lived in the world of light, you might have scoffed at such a thing. Now nothing seems impossible.

Your new friend, Sarah, shares her sleeping spot on the floor with you. A week passes, without word from Nell. The meagre prison rations leave a gnawing hole of hunger in your stomach, and you start to curse yourself for being so foolish. Nell's not coming back. The seemingly unending days at the window, the frigid nights spent huddled on the floor, and the constant human stink begin to wipe hope and memory from your mind...

Another week later, however, on the night of a full moon, after you have given up all hope of a

response, Nell returns. In your sleep, you hear one of her rhymes floating into the cell, repeating again and again: *Little birdie, fly to me, and we will have our liberty.*

The words wind their way into your dreams until you wake. You creep over to the window and thrust your face up towards her weathered one peering through the bars. She's close enough that you can smell her breath. It's hot and vinegary.

'You're back!' you whisper.

'Bet you're wondering what I know,' she hisses. 'For it's been slow, unpicking the thread of whispers...Can you hear?'

'Hear what?' you ask.

'A plan,' she whispers. 'Tick tock, tick tock, hit the gaoler with a rock. You want to be free, little birdie? Your da's the key. But you have to trust Nell. Are you ready, little daughter?'

'Da has a plan for me to escape?' you gasp.

Nell nods feverishly. Her eyes are aglow.

'But what's his sentence?' you ask. 'Will he be transported?'

Nell closes her eyes, and shakes her head slowly. 'Sentenced to hang, he'll never be free. He'll swing by his neck, unless you use the key!'

A sob escapes your throat. 'No!' you cry. You don't want to believe her. 'Is it really true?'

Nell makes a noise like a cat preparing to fight. It makes the hairs on your neck stand on end. She points a gnarled finger at you.

'Trust makes power, and the power makes trust. Blood feeds water, and the water feeds dust,' she hisses. Then she looks into your face and smiles cunningly. 'Green Ireland beckons you home to the nest. But she'll only take the best. What'll it be? Give Nelly your biggest treasure and fly free? Or wait, wait, wait in Hell till the noose is tied with Da's neck inside?'

Your heart pounds even harder. You look around the cell in despair. Fly free? How could Nell possibly get me out of here? And even if she could, is that really Da's plan? What if she's lying to me?

You imagine Da waiting in the dark belly of his prison hulk, plotting to escape and hoping to fly with you to freedom. You can't bear the thought of letting him down – of not even trying to see him one last time. But then you imagine something else: what if Nell doesn't know Da's sentence at all, has never even talked to him, and is just spinning a web of lies and guesswork?

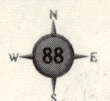

If you try to escape and you're caught, there'll be no mercy for you or Da this time – you'd both be certain to hang. It's a big risk. But perhaps anything's better than wasting away in gaol while time runs out for your da...

✱ To trust Nell and attempt to escape, go to page 89.
✱ To decide you don't trust her, and stay in prison for now, go to page 100.

'All right, Nell,' you say. 'If you can get me out of here, I'll pay you well. But how are you going to do it? What's the plan?'

'A promise, a pact, no turning back!'

'Very well, then, I promise. But what—'

'Leave it with Nell! And never tell. Don't whisper a word, little bird, and you'll see the way to flee very soon.'

She scampers away into the night.

ALTHOUGH YOU CAN'T tell anyone about your escape plan, you decide to talk to Sarah about the idea – without telling her any of the details. You hope that she might want to escape with you.

'I'd never try to escape,' she says adamantly. 'There was a woman in here who tried it once – she smuggled herself out in a basket of laundry. When they caught her and dumped her back in here, they'd beat her so badly that...' Sarah shudders. 'We tried to look after her. But she died a few days later.' Sarah suddenly narrows her eyes. 'You haven't been talking to Nell again, have you?'

'No,' you lie, and you say no more on the subject.

EVERY NIGHT THAT week, Nell comes back while the other women are sleeping, and the two of you take turns in using a file she brings with her to work away at the stone around the edge of one of the bars in the window. Very slowly, the bar begins to wriggle and loosen. If the footsteps of a guard ever approach, Nell and her file dissolve into the darkness as fast as a wink.

On the tenth night of filing, the bar finally comes loose and Nell yanks you upwards through the hole, onto the street. You stand under the star-filled sky and the air around you feels so wondrously big that you almost burst into tears.

You and Nell begin sprinting down the street. There is not a soul in sight, and the only sound is your footsteps slapping the cobblestones. Laughter wells up inside you. You're free! You want to shout and dance.

Nell stops to catch her breath, and you throw

your arms around her. You even kiss her sunken cheek. 'Thank you, Nell!' you cry.

A surprised smile comes over Nell's weathered old face. 'Little birdie,' she chuckles, touching the spot on her cheek where you kissed her. 'You're kind to Nell.'

'Yes, and there's more,' you say, reaching down for the hem of your petticoat. You find the lump of the bracelet in the hem and guide it to Nell's fingertips. 'Feel that? That's my greatest treasure – a beautiful bracelet of gold and jewels. When I see my da again, you can have it!'

Nell looks awestruck. 'Little birdie has *another* treasure she wants to give to Nell? But Nell can't tell... She made a mistake. She shouldn't take...' She trails off, seeming edgy all of a sudden.

'Wait a minute, Nell,' you say. 'What do you mean, *another* treasure? What's the mistake?'

Around a corner is a parked carriage with a strong-looking white horse attached. A man in a suit steps out of the shiny black carriage, takes your arm and, before you know it, hoists you up the step and onto the seat inside.

Nell follows, her face crinkled in worry. The man in the suit leaps in and sits beside her. Then the driver closes the door behind you with a *click*, and the carriage begins moving down the dark street at a brisk pace.

You've never been inside a carriage before – they're only for rich people. This one has glass windows and padded seats, but you scarcely take in the luxury. Your mind is a whirl of questions.

'Who are you?' you ask the man in the suit. 'Where are we going?'

'My name is Doctor Giles,' says the man. His hands are pale and neat. The gold chain of a fob watch trails from his waistcoat pocket. 'And I believe we're going to find your father, isn't that right? But first, a toast. To your freedom!'

He takes a dark-brown glass bottle from his inside pocket and pours a small measure into a little metal tumbler. A strong whiff of rum fills the carriage. He passes you the cup, and you look at it suspiciously.

'Come now,' says Doctor Giles. 'You wouldn't be so prudish as to refuse a little nip, would you?'

You *do* want to refuse the doctor's drink. You don't understand who he is, why a rich doctor would make a pastime of picking up escaped convicts in the middle of the night, or how on earth he knows

Nell. But a cautious voice inside you tells you to play along. You're in his carriage, at his mercy – best to just pretend to do as he asks, and try to learn what is going on here.

You lift the cup to your lips. The smell burns its way up your nostrils as you tip your head back and pretend to take a big sip. But your lips remain tightly closed.

'Good girl,' says the doctor. 'Drink up, now.' He reaches below the seat and gets out a dark red blanket, which he spreads over your knee. 'It's a long trip. Have a rest, if you'd like.'

You realise that it's not just rum in this cup – when you lick your lips, you can taste not only the alcohol, but something nastily bitter, disguised with a lot of dissolved sugar. You pretend to drink again and then, with the doctor watching keenly, you make a big show of letting your eyes droop and your head become heavy, until you curl up under the blanket, ready to listen for every clue and plan your next move.

For a while, there is no sound except the drumming of the horse's hooves and rattle of the carriage. Then Doctor Giles's voice says: 'She's a nice specimen, Nell. Excellent work.'

A shudder runs over your skin. What does he mean by *specimen*?

Nell's voice sounds grumpy when she replies: 'Nelly wants...to let the little birdie go.'

'What?' Giles sounds confused and annoyed. 'That's out of the question, Nell. Don't tell me you've become fond of her!'

'Little birdie was kind to Nell,' she says sulkily. 'Said she'd give Nelly the treasure from her skirt... Nell doesn't want her hurt...'

'She won't feel a thing, Nell, you know that. And when we arrive I'll pay you what I promised *and* you can have the treasure from her skirt, whatever it is.' Giles sounds outright exasperated now.

Under the blanket, your hands curl into fists. You don't know what the doctor is planning, but it's definitely not to take you to Da. Nell is to be *paid* for having delivered you to this man.

'Nelly can bring you more dead ones, bodies from the graves, as many as the doctor needs...' she wheedles.

Your heart beats in your mouth.

'They are of no use to me anymore – too stiff and decayed,' Giles barks back. 'To complete my research it's vital I use a live subject. Listen, Nell,' –

his voice drops to a persuasive murmur – 'there are endless poor wretches like this one clogging up our city. Her life would have been a complete waste, but in my hands, she will *mean* something. She will be crucial in the advancement of medical science.'

As understanding dawns on you, you have to fight not to throw up. Nell is a graverobber – one of the criminals you've heard about who take bodies out of graves and sell them to medical schools for dissection. But this doctor, Giles, is no longer satisfied with corpses that have been dead for days. He's persuaded Nell to bring him a living person – *you* – who he can knock out with whatever was in that cup, and then... well, you can't bear to think of what he would do next.

Wild panic gallops through your brain. You realise you've begun shaking violently, and you squeeze your muscles up tight before anyone notices that you're not drugged fast asleep. Your breath is coming in fast gulps. You want to scream, but you keep your lips tightly pressed together, the silent shriek whirling like a tornado through your mind. You have to work out what to do.

You're in a fast-moving carriage – you'd hurt yourself badly if you tried to leap out. You're furious at Nell's betrayal, but the doctor is your biggest enemy. Will you have the strength to fight him? Or would you have a better chance of getting away once the carriage has stopped? You open your eye just a chink and see the doctor taking something from his bag that looks like a rope. You realise you may not be able to get away from him once the carriage stops.

With that realisation, you move with such strength and speed it's as if a spirit has taken hold of your body. You grab the blanket in each hand and leap from the seat, throwing your full weight against the doctor and managing to wrap the blanket over his head and neck. Nell squirms out of the way as he falls across the seat. You pin him down with your knees but he's fighting to get up, and he's much stronger than you are. You let go of the blanket and grip the seat with your hands, trying to keep him pinned down.

He starts shouting, 'Smith! Stop the carriage! *Smith!*'

But his voice is cut short – Nell has grabbed the blanket, and she's smothering him with it. She gives you a wild grin, but you feel sickened by her glee.

'You lying witch,' you snarl. 'You never even spoke to Da!' But Nell doesn't hear you. Her face is gripped with ecstasy.

'Snuff the candle, pluck the flower. Choke his breath and take his power,' she chants.

The doctor's limbs are windmilling, thumping the walls and floor of the carriage. The driver must have noticed something is amiss, because the carriage slows down. You don't want to stay in here and help Nell to commit a murder. You just want to get as far away from both of them as possible. Judging that you could jump from the carriage at this speed, you leap up and grab the doorhandle. But it has been locked from the outside!

The doctor throws Nell off him with a roar and makes a grab for you. Just at that moment, however, the door is opened from the outside, and you push your way past the driver into the night air.

A quick glance down the street tells you there's nowhere to hide: on one side is the River Thames, on the other a long row of mansions with high gates. The driver clutches at you, but you duck just in time. Thumps and shrieks from the carriage tell you that Nell has attacked the doctor once again.

The driver leans inside the carriage, and when he re-emerges he's holding a musket. He shouts at Nell, 'Stop or I'll shoot!'

You look up and see the big horse harnessed to

the carriage. You leap up onto his back, keeping your knees above the long wooden shafts that connect the horse to the carriage. Then you dig your knees in, lean forward, and give him a slap to get him moving.

'Faster! Come on!' you urge into his ear and, as if he understands you, the horse begins galloping at full speed, the carriage rattling behind you, its open door swinging and banging, the driver running alongside with his gun, trying to keep up.

The horse's muscles ripple under you like a wave. Gripping his wide girth with your knees, you lean over and use your hands to start unbuckling the straps that connect him to the shaft.

You don't want to pull this carriage around anymore, do you? you think to the horse. *You want to be free. You deserve to be free.*

Just then, you hear a bang from the driver's gun, and a searing pain rips through your shoulder. Gasping, you manage to swing yourself upright, and you grab hold of your shoulder with one hand. Blood trickles through your fingers. Your breath gushes in and out in time with the horse's as his hooves drum against the cobblestones. The carriage still bounces along behind you.

You're starting to feel faint. You manage to lie down along the horse's neck and bury your face in his mane. His body starts to feel as though it's swaying under you, and you try to grip more tightly with your knees, but there's no strength left in them.

You look sideways, to the River Thames. The moonlight is shining on the water. You shoulder is throbbing, but you feel an elated sense of peace.

'This is what freedom tastes like,' you whisper to the horse. 'Remember this.'

Then there's another *bang* as the gun fires again, and a burning pain in your back, so intense you can barely breathe. The world narrows to a tiny spot of light, and you tumble from the horse's back into the darkness.

✴ To return to your last choice and try again, go to page 88.

You've decided: you've had enough of Nell and her strange ways. You can only hope that Da wasn't really planning an escape, because the thought of letting him down is devastating.

'I won't do it, Nell,' you say, with more certainty than you really feel. 'I know you've never seen Da – you're just making it up.'

Nell spits in your face. You turn your back on her. As you furiously wipe the warm slime away, you hear her scuttling down the road, muttering, 'Little birdie knew Nell lied, even though Nell tried, she tried...'

You feel a weight lift from your chest now that you're no longer certain that Da will be hanged. It seems Nell was spinning stories, after all.

Sarah was right, you think, fuming. *I was mad to even trust her with my twopence, let alone my life.*

'You've made the right choice,' Sarah says kindly the next day when you tell her what happened.

'She made up your da's sentence to frighten you. The mad old hunchback's just cross you aren't swallowing her lies and supplying her with any more money.'

You hope she's right. You know no more about Da's future for certain than you did when you saw him being led to the Old Bailey.

'Now I'll have to wait and see, and hope for the best,' you say. You shrug and smile.

'I'd like to believe you could start a new life with your da someday,' Sarah said wistfully. 'That would make me happy.'

She looks so forlorn. 'What's the matter?' you ask, shaking her shoulder. 'You're speaking as if you'll never be free yourself!'

'I won't,' she says quietly. 'I'm to be transported for life.'

You feel a sense of dread begin to creep over you. Sarah's never told you why she's in here. What could she have done that would be awful enough to get her a life sentence?

'Sarah?' you ask. 'What is it?'

Sarah is pale-faced, her hands clasped in her lap. She won't look at you. Your stomach starts to hurt

a little. How in the world have you not asked Sarah about this before now?

'I think it's time I tell you the truth,' she says softly.

✦ To continue with the story, go to page 103.

Sarah sighs heavily. 'I wish my da had loved me as much as yours does,' she begins. 'Perhaps he did when I was just a baby. But in all my memories of him, his only love was a bottle of liquor. Every scrap of money we made, it went to the tavern. Six children, he and Ma had together, and all of us hungry from sun-up to sun-down. Half of what he spent on rum could have bought us a meal, but the alcohol had such a spell over him, he'd let his own family starve before he'd give up drinking.'

'I'm so sorry,' you say. It feels like a cold wind is blowing through your chest.

'I used to wish that he'd drink himself to death – that he'd fall into the river in a stupor one night, or that his guts would go bad and kill him. But in the end... I was the one who killed him.'

You gasp. Your mind is reeling. Good, kind Sarah, a murderer?

'I didn't mean to,' she confesses. 'One night, he came back late, raging like a storm. He started beating Ma, as he often did, but this time he

knocked her out cold. The little ones were screaming, and he came towards us next. I had to make him stop. There was a bottle there. I threw it at his head,' she whispers sadly. 'I wasn't trying to kill him – I just wanted him to stop. But they said it was murder.'

You pull Sarah into a tight embrace. You can't believe that she had to go through something so awful. You feel her hot tears on your shoulder, and you whisper fiercely into her hair, 'If I'd been there, I'd have killed him for hurting you.'

Sarah draws back, wipes her tears, and manages a wan smile. 'My family's not even better off without him – not now that I've gone too. I was lucky not to hang for it; in the end, they ruled it was "accidental" – but that was still enough to get me a life sentence. The other children are still too young to work much, so now earning is all up to Ma. She's all alone. They're not being beaten, at least, but I just wish I could help.'

'Most of the prisoners in here only think of themselves,' you declare, 'and you're here wishing you could help others. You're an angel, Sarah MacBride.'

She gives you another little smile.

'I think you deserve some good luck at last, and I know just what's going to happen,' you tell her. You begin to imagine a future for the two of you, with such conviction that it feels as if it really will come true. 'I'll be sentenced to transportation too, and we'll sail across the world side by side. We'll finish our time as convicts and put all that behind us. We'll receive a parcel of land and farm it together. Shall we farm fruit trees, or have horses?'

'Both.' Sarah grins. You can see the light growing in her eyes.

'All right then, so we shall,' you agree. 'If you have any of your sentence left to serve, we'll tell that damn Governor, or whoever's in charge, that you're to be assigned to me, and we'll live together as sisters. Our horses will be famed throughout the colony, and we'll send the extra money to your ma and the little ones. My da will be free by then too. He can join us.'

Sarah's laughing and shaking her head. 'Don't you disbelieve me, Sarah MacBride,' you scold her. 'That's exactly how it will happen, wait and see.' You reach out and squeeze her hand, and then you whisper, 'I promise with all my heart that no matter what happens, you're family to me.'

Sarah kisses your cheek. 'And you to me,' she replies.

ANOTHER MONTH LATER, you and Sarah are sitting in the quadrangle near your cell with the sewing circle you've recently joined, each of you working on sewing a quilt made from fabric scraps brought in by a charitable visitor called Miss Townsend, who's today's helper, here to teach you to sew. It's spring now, not so cold, but you're still looking forward to having a second blanket to call your own.

A clanging door and heavy footsteps cause everyone to lift their heads up from their sewing. A guard enters the room and calls your name. You slip, and stab your fingertip with the needle.

Feeling your stomach flip, you put down your quilt and stand. This is it. It's your turn to be taken away for sentencing at the courthouse.

A circle of worried and sympathetic eyes look up at you.

'Be brave, dear,' says Miss Townsend. 'Remember, they can take your freedom away, but never your dignity.'

A few of the other prisoners snort under their

breath. Everyone here except Miss Townsend knows what it feels like to be stripped of dignity. You look at Sarah. She gives you an encouraging nod and a strong smile that says: *You can do this*.

Led by a chain attached to iron cuffs on your wrists, you are taken deep into the tunnels below Newgate. One of these tunnels leads to the Old Bailey courthouse, where a judge will pronounce your fate. This day has been hanging over you for two months now. *I don't want to die*, you think desperately. *I want to live. I want to see Da again. Please.*

At the end of the tunnel is a flight of stairs. You pause at the bottom, your stomach churning. Fear has made your whole body so weak that suddenly you're not sure if you can even manage to climb them.

The gaolor gives your chain a yank. You take a deep breath, and dig down inside yourself for some courage. Then you begin to climb, one foot after the other.

THIS IS IT: the moment you'll find out if you will live, or die at the end of a rope.

The judge looks down on you from the bench. He has a large red nose covered with little red veins, a horsehair wig, and very tired-looking eyes. From time to time, his fingers slip under his wig to scratch at his head.

You suddenly wonder how you must look to him. While you've awaited your sentencing in gaol, you've become weak and withered from lack of sunlight and decent food. You feel so thin that you almost fancy there wouldn't be enough weight on you to pull down the noose and hang you: you might just slip from the rope and float away, like an autumn leaf.

Still, you remember that where there's life, there's hope, and that you aren't hanged yet.

You've heard that judges sometimes show mercy to young people who show regret for their crimes. You look up into this judge's face and will your voice not to wobble.

'I'm truly sorry for what I did, sir,' you say. 'I know it was wrong. I've learnt my lesson, sir, please believe me.'

The judge sighs. He shakes his head solemnly. You don't know if he is disappointed in you, or sorry for you, or simply fed up with his job.

He rubs his brow. 'I see criminals come before me day in, day out,' he muses, almost as if to himself, 'and they seem to be getting younger and skinnier by the week. How old are you?'

'Thirteen, sir,' you whisper.

The judge harrumphs. Then he nods. 'I don't believe there is any lesson to be learned in hanging one whose life has barely begun. Better to give some of you young ones a chance to prosper in a new place, where you can prove yourself with some hard, honest work. You are hereby sentenced to be transported for seven years beyond the seas.'

There's a knock of the judge's hammer, and a murmuring and shuffling of feet as a guard leads you from the room. Your mind is whirling, and relief floods through you. *Seven years beyond the seas!* You've been given the shortest term possible for transportation. So, you're not to die... but to be blown like a leaf to another world.

'I wouldn't be looking so happy if I were you,' scoffs the warden who leads you out of the courtroom. 'You're going to the end of the earth – full of naught but thieves and murderers. Now get a bloody move on.'

As you are led back down the tunnel to Newgate,

the tapping of your hem against your leg reminds you of the bracelet, still sewn securely inside.

You remember the feeling of courage you had on the day it was given to you, when you calmed the horse. *I'll need even more courage for the years to come*, you think.

You remember, too, the lady's words: *Keep this, close and secret... When you understand its meaning, you'll know it's time to pass it on.* You still don't know what that meaning is, but you're determined that you'll keep your treasure with you for the voyage and the new life to come.

THE MONTHS DRAG by in prison as you wait for your name to be called up. You've have no word from Da, but there have been no hangings since you saw him, either. *Is he, even now, sailing across the world in chains?* you wonder. *How will I ever find him again?*

Every few months, rumours fly as another shipload of prisoners prepares to leave England, but it never seems to be your or Sarah's turn... until one summer's morning, a guard appears on your level of the prison and begins shouting out a list of convicts

to be transported to the southern colony of Van Diemen's Land on the next ship. You all watch him anxiously through the bars.

'Sarah MacBride,' he barks. Sarah gives a little gasp and squeezes your hand.

Your heart beats in your mouth. Will your name be on the list too? You can't survive in this place without your only friend. The list seems to go on forever: twenty, thirty, forty names. *Oh please, God,* you beg. *Please.* But the gaolor finishes reading. He hasn't called your name.

Sarah looks at you in desperation, tears in her eyes. 'I don't want to go to Australia without you,' she whispers.

You are trying to smile; to be glad for her sake. You want to say something consoling – that you won't be far behind – but you can't make the words come out.

Then the gaoler flips the paper over. He's just noticed one more name written on the back. It's yours.

✦ In this matter, you have no choice. Go to Page 112.

You should be used to suffering by now, having spent near two seasons in the hell that was Newgate. But the way this new prison of yours – the ship that will take you to the colony of Van Diemen's Land – pitches and heaves like a beast having bad dreams is disturbing to all on board.

I won't throw up, you tell yourself that first morning. *I have a stomach of iron.* But, one by one, all the women around you below deck – including Sarah – are beginning to retch, and the smell in these closed quarters is acrid and foul.

Pressing your lips together tightly and trying to concentrate on something else, you wipe Sarah's hair from her sweaty brow and describe for her how you picture your arrival to the colony in your mind's eye.

'They'll let us up on deck to get our first glimpse of the shore. We'll be able to smell the fresh salt air and hear the gulls – or perhaps they don't have gulls down there, but far more beautiful seabirds with red and golden feathers. As we approach the land, a beam of light will break through the clouds, falling

upon our ship as if it were our mothers' hands touching us, bidding us welcome to our new home.

'All the folk of the colony will blow us kisses as we sail into shore. And the kangaroos will be hopping around, all excited because they've heard we're coming and they want to be our pets!'

Sarah can't help but laugh, although it makes her cough and retch again. 'A kangaroo for a pet? You say some wild things! How do you know they're not vicious?'

'Oh, they're gentle as bunnies – I'm told they come right up to you and give you flowers. Strange Australian flowers that smell of honey and are as purple as a king's cloak…'

Your story gives you and Sarah something to hold on to – a rope in your hands that might just stretch all the way to the other side of the world.

The ship begins to rise and plunge through the waves even more robustly, its timbers squeaking and its masts groaning like ghosts. Bilge water and vomit are lapping about on the floor, and you won't be let out on deck until the morning. It seems impossible that you will learn to sleep, eat and walk about on this ship – but you must, for your journey will take four months at least.

Out on deck the next morning, there is not a skerrick of land in sight, just pale waves all around you. For someone used to the confined spaces of alleyways, cramped hovels and gaols, even to be able to stand up straight without knocking your head on something is wonderful. The salty breeze reminds you of your old life back in Ireland, and the world is so wide all around you, as if it has been unfolded from a cardboard box into a huge sheet of clean white paper.

You straighten up, thinking: *Hello world, this is me.* Excitement dances in your chest, like light on the waves.

From talking to the other prisoners, you've found out that, as you have a seven-year sentence, you might be given what they call a 'ticket of leave' after only four years of work. Then you'll be able to earn a wage for your work and have a bit more freedom. Sarah, as she has a life sentence, will have to be on her best behaviour for ten whole years before she may be granted a ticket of leave – but your lives as free women seem within reach.

You think of the bracelet snuggled in your hem, and you try to remember the colour and order of the gemstones. You're pretty sure that the rainbow stone was next to the raspberry-red one, then the two stones as green as fresh grass, followed by the clear and the black ones next to each other, and lastly a stone as dark-green as a fir tree. *When you understand its meaning, you'll know it's time to pass it on*, the lady said. What did she mean?

Your thoughts are interrupted by the strangest feeling that someone is staring at you. You turn around, and you are right – a sailor is looking at you. He has the brownest skin you've ever seen, and his eyes are black and shiny as river stones. He wears a cap and has a long, wiry beard. He nods and smiles, showing broken teeth, and you can't help but smile back.

'Tsk!' a woman says bossily into your ear. 'Don't look at the lascars!'

You turn to see a woman, in convict dress as you are, pursing her lips as haughtily as a queen.

'What's a lascar?' you ask.

'That man is one! Sailors from foreign lands. They're here to do the cooking and cleaning, tend the animals and so on.'

'Animals?' you ask eagerly. 'What kinds of animals?'

The bossy lady rolls her eyes, as if she's been at sea for years and can barely bother to inform a simpleton like you of the facts. Then she says:

'Haven't you heard them from time to time? The free settlers on our ship are bringing them out to the colonies. There are a few dozen chickens, and even a horse, I believe.'

A horse! You resolve to search out the lascar and make him your friend. You catch his eye and wave. He cheerfully waves back.

'Stop that!' snaps the woman. 'There's no point in talking to them – they speak some other language, and what's more' – she drops her voice, scandalised – 'they pray to a *different* god. Imagine it! If I were captain of this ship, I certainly wouldn't let any heathens aboard.'

'Well, it's lucky you're just convict scum like the rest of us then, isn't it,' you retort. The woman's face turns red as a beetroot. But you're not finished yet. 'I'd much rather talk to that lascar than you – even if he doesn't speak English, I've a feeling he'd make more sense than you.'

The woman gives an outraged 'harrumph!' and storms away.

You catch the lascar's eye again, and impulsively you make a neighing sound, pointing at him and nodding.

At first, he looks utterly perplexed. Then he

breaks into a grin and starts nodding too. He gestures to the hold of the ship, below deck at the front, and makes the neighing sound back to you. Then he chuckles.

You can't stop smiling.

YOU AND THE rest of the convicts are put to work in shifts every day, scrubbing decks. It's tough labour – but no tougher than other work you've done before.

One part of your day that you look forward to is the school lessons. Some of the convicts who can read and write are appointed as teachers to the ones, like you, who can't. You never had a chance to go to school, and you're pleased that you'll arrive in Australia knowing your letters and numbers.

A few days into your journey, the lascar picks you out of your working group.

'Need work...animals,' he tells your overseer, and he leads you across the deck. 'You like horse?' he asks you.

'Oh yes!'

'Horse poo?'

'Oh! Well...'

He laughs. 'My name Amal. You help with animals. Yes?'

'All right,' you agree. You climb through a trapdoor in the deck, down some steep stairs, into the animals' enclosure. The stale air reeks of manure and animal sweat. You see chickens in cages against one wall, and in the back pen, a lovely female palomino horse. You gasp.

You and Amal get to work mucking manure out of her pen and grooming her. Although the horse stands on the ground, a kind of hammock goes around her body to cradle her and help her keep balanced as the ship rises and falls. As you look at the hammock, you can't help but notice her huge round belly.

You ask Amal: 'Is there...' – you think of how to phrase it in simple English – 'a baby in there?'

He grins. 'Yes! She is mother. Baby coming in two month.'

AFTER A FEW weeks of this work, the horse, who you've named Betty, has bonded with you: she whinnies happily even just hearing your footsteps and voice coming down the stairs with Amal.

'When baby horse comes,' says Amal, 'very

dangerous. Mother, baby, maybe die. You can help?'

Oh Lord, you think. You don't know the first thing about birth or foals. You can't believe Amal would trust a convict girl to help in a life-and-death situation – but he knows and trusts you now, and so does Betty. There's no way you'll let either of them down.

'I'll be there,' you say.

FIVE WEEKS LATER, a storm is tossing the boat about like a rabbit in a dog's mouth. Women are holding on to their narrow bunks and moaning. No one is sleeping tonight.

The hatch that leads up to deck is firmly padlocked shut from the outside. It's almost pitch-black down here, but it's noisy: as well as the moans, there is thunder, sailors shouting, timbers groaning and waves slapping the hull. But there's something else, too: an inhuman screaming that makes the hairs on your neck stand on end. There's a distant clattering of hooves, then another drawn-out scream, which you realise must be Betty – and that she must be in the throes of giving birth!

You can't bear to think of Betty going through

this without you, but the only way out of here would be to break open the trapdoor and make your way across the stormy deck above to the hold.

'Sarah,' you exclaim, leaning up to the bunk above you, 'would you help me to break out of here, if I asked? I told Amal that I'd help him with Betty when she gave birth, and just *listen*.'

Sarah reaches down and grips your hand. 'Amal will come and get you if he needs you,' she says firmly. 'Betty will be all right. And besides, you'd be caught or blown overboard, and I'm not sure which one would be worse.'

Sarah is always the sensible one, and usually you admire her for this, but at this moment, you want to shake her.

I promised Amal and Betty that I'd be there, you think. *Now what will I do?*

✦ If you try to break out and reach Amal and Betty, go to page 121.

✦ If you remain where you are, locked below deck, go to page 125.

Initially it's a relief to decide that you'll break out and go to Betty and Amal's aid, but you soon realise you're going to have a huge challenge just getting to the hatch exit on the other side of the room in this storm.

Your mind is made up, though. Soon you're on your hands and knees on the hard wooden floor, wrist-deep in churning black water, which soaks your stockings and dress. The ship lurches and you are thrown sideways into a bunk. Your head slams against the wood, and its occupant shouts in fright. With the ship's next lurch, you are thrown forward, tumbling across to the other side of the hull, landing with a *thump* at the base of the ladder leading to the hatch.

You grab the ladder before you can tumble away from it again, and begin to climb. The ladder tips back and forth as if it's trying to throw you off. When you reach the top, you hang on like grim death, your breath coming in noisy gasps. You can't really spare a hand to let go and even try to get the trapdoor open. Its timber is thick as a man's arm, and its hinges are iron.

The woman who sleeps on the top bunk nearest the hatch reaches out and taps your arm. In the darkness, you feel her press a metal teaspoon into your hand. You don't know where she would have found such a thing.

'Break us all out of here, love,' she moans. 'I want to breathe fresh air before I die in this storm.'

You get to work with the handle of the spoon, hacking away at the timber close to the hinges, which seems a little splintered and damp. If you can break the hinge, despite the outer padlock being locked fast on the other side, perhaps you can open the trapdoor from its hinged side instead. Trying to concentrate on this job in the rolling storm is making you feel giddy.

Thump! You brace yourself against the ladder and try to slam the trapdoor upwards with your shoulder. *Thump!* It seems to be giving way a little around the hinges where you have loosened it with your spoon. Your shoulder is throbbing. Every now and again, you catch the sound of Betty's neighs, which spurs you on. The other convicts have taken interest and are either cheering you on

or telling you to stop being a damned fool and get back to your bunk. With all their yelling and your thumping of the trapdoor, it's become very loud in here.

Suddenly you hear footsteps coming towards the trapdoor and a key turning in its padlock. The door opens and an officer's face peers in at you.

'What on earth is the meaning of—' he begins.

A convict screams: 'Go for your life, girl!' and you see your chance. You heave your way onto the deck and scramble past the officer.

Salt water slaps you in the face.

'Hey!' he shouts.

You stagger in the direction of the hold at the front of the ship. You can hear panicked neighing.

'I'm coming, Betty!' you shout, but the wind snatches away your words.

The boat reaches the peak of a wave. You feel a moment of weightlessness, then the deck plunges below your feet. The officer snatches at your arm but misses. You hit the deck and a crescendo of foam crashes over it, sweeping you uncontrollably towards its tilting edge, your arms flailing around for a rope or anything to grab hold of. You smack into the railings at the edge of the deck, and then

cold, black water rises up and sweeps you under the railing and down into the depths.

It is strangely quiet underwater. You are dragged down, deeper and deeper. You kick for all you're worth, but it makes no difference. The hull of the ship, way above you, is drifting out of sight. The water is pressing in on your eardrums, tighter and tighter. You feel you are going to pop with the effort of holding air in your lungs. Your chest is burning.

Helplessly, you let go. The air bubbles out of you, and water rushes into your lungs. You watch your breath float away from you. Your body will never be found.

THE END

✦ To return to your last choice and try again, go to page 120.

'Of course, you're right. What would I do without you to calm me down, Sarah?' you sigh, letting your head fall back against your bunk. Your bed lurches under you; you have to grip the sides to stop from falling out.

'Get yourself killed in some harebrained mission, no doubt,' she says warmly. 'I'm sure it'd give all these convict ladies a laugh to see you try to break out of here in the middle of a storm, but I'd rather have you alive, thanks.'

You love Sarah so. She reminds you of your older sister, Erin, who was also reassuring and level-headed. Thinking now of her terrible death by childbirth gives you the shivers. You wonder if Betty is as scared and helpless as Erin was.

Aloud, you say, 'Hurry up, Amal. I'm ready.'

Your bunk is the other end of the room from the hatch, and you are clinging to it so tightly that you don't notice it open, until a woman from the other end of the room shouts your name.

'God himself knows why,' she shouts, as rain pelts

through the opened hatch and into the room, 'but there's a lascar here says he needs your help with a horse!'

Your heart lifts. You crawl and stagger your way towards the ladder, as the ship pitches beneath you.

Up on deck, Amal gives you his arm. You are drenched to the skin in the short time it takes you both to hobble across the deck and into the stable hold.

The air in the hold is even thicker than usual with the stench of sweat and urine-soaked hay. Betty's eyes are flashing and her nostrils are flaring. You stand at her side in her pen, trying to reassure her as the floor tilts violently underneath you. Amal directs you to help him unclip the hammock around Betty's body so that she can lie down to deliver her foal.

As you get the hammock away, Betty's hooves clatter, and suddenly her full weight falls against you. With an *oof*, you brace yourself against the wall behind you and help to ease her down to the floor. Her terrified neighs stop then, and she begins huffing and straining. Amal wipes down Betty's body with a damp cloth.

'What kind of fool horse has her baby in a storm, now?' you murmur to her, but you mean it lovingly.

'This baby didn't want to wait till a sensible time, did it? It's all right, it's all right, Betty, my dear.'

Her furry ears swivel towards you. You keep talking, as it seems to soothe her. You kneel beside her and brace yourself against her sweaty flanks as you ride out the rise and plunge of the waves.

'What kind of horse will this be, now?' you ask her. 'Not an English horse; and not an Australian horse, either. It must be... a seahorse! Let's meet this lovely little seahorse. Come on, now, you can do it...'

Betty's huffs continue, mingling with the sound of waves crashing against the hull. Gradually, something slippery and purple emerges from her.

You take hold of two slimy hooves while Amal supports the foal's head, and then you pull until, suddenly, the foal gushes out onto the straw. It is covered in a sack of wrinkly white film, like the skin that forms on the top of hot milk. It is so floppy that it looks dead.

Amal starts working frantically to clear the little foal's airways. A lump rises in your throat. *Please let it live – please!*

The storm continues to rage. Betty doesn't get up. She has closed her eyes. She seems to be losing a lot of blood.

'Take the cloth!' shouts Amal. 'Betty maybe die! Please, you take and stop blood hard!'

He is holding a wad of cloth out towards you. You press it against Betty, under her tail where the foal came out. Her blood is running along your arm, soaking your dress. You feel like you might faint, but you tell yourself to pull it together.

You press harder. The bleeding slows. You let out a slow, shaky breath. You croon to Betty, steadily, gently, struggling all the while to keep your balance. Betty opens her eyes and looks at you.

Amal is doing well with the foal. It lifts its head and blinks its eyes. He manages, on his knees, to gently bring the gooey, gangly thing up towards Betty's head, and she starts to lick it.

Amal is laughing and nearly sobbing at the same time. 'This horse want to kill everybody,' he laughs. 'Storm and baby together, so much trouble!'

He looks at you intently.

'Tonight, we pray very hard for this. You pray Jesus, I pray Allah. We say, "Thank you. We live, mother live, baby live."'

He takes the cloth from you and checks the bleeding. It has stopped.

'Very good.'

Betty and her foal are alive because of you and Amal. *Whatever bad choices I've made up until now*, you think, *my life has been worth it, because of this. I count for something.* It's the first time in a long time that you can remember feeling this way.

THREE MONTHS LATER, the foal – who you and Amal have agreed to call Baraka, meaning 'blessed' in Amal's language – is standing and walking happily, eating as much hay as he can get and feeding greedily from Betty.

You are down in the hold, petting Baraka, when you hear a whoop of excitement from passengers on the deck. You rush up the stairs to see a blue stripe on the horizon: Van Diemen's Land, your final port.

Your stomach lurches as you suddenly realise you may not see Betty, Baraka or Amal ever again once your ship lands. Amal will sail off on his next voyage. Betty and Baraka will go, hopefully, to a green pasture with a kind master.

You remember the day you promised Sarah that, when you made your new life in Van Diemen's Land, you'd live together as sisters. Your heart grows heavy as you realise it's probably an impossible

promise to keep. You'll each be assigned to different masters, most likely, and be put to hard toil, possibly hundreds of miles apart. Gaining your ticket of leave might not be easy – especially for Sarah. How will you find each other after all that time?

Your throat clenches. The voyage has been tough – at times hellish – but right now, you can't bear for it to end.

Three hours later, you and Sarah sit together on your bunk, holding hands, listening to the thumps and thuds of the ship docking.

'We'll be together again soon enough,' she murmurs.

You bite your lip and rub a tear away with your shoulder. 'Right you are,' you tell her. 'We crossed the world together – nothing can break our bond.'

✦ In this matter you have no choice. Go to page 131.

Although you have now arrived at Hobart Town, you are held on board the ship for a further four days. Government officials come to interview you about your skills and your history, and they record every detail of your physical appearance. When you at last leave the ship, before dawn on the fifth day, you're marched up to the Hobart Town gaol. It's not as big as Newgate, but inside it's just as crowded and dank. It gives you the shivers to hear the door slam and the key turn in the lock.

By the end of the week, a middle-aged man with a tidy moustache and wearing a top hat and a brown jacket comes to the gaol to take you away. He looks you up and down – you feel like a sheep at a market – then he signs a paper and leads you out of the cell. You cast a frantic farewell glance over your shoulder at Sarah, who is trying not to cry.

As the ox-and-cart rattles slowly away from Hobart Town, the man speaks to you, briskly but not unkindly: 'My name is Mr Tilsome,' he says, 'but you will call me "sir".'

'Yes, sir,' you reply immediately.

'We've quite the journey back to Bothwell – two days, if the weather stays fine. Though after so many months on a ship, I don't suppose that will bother you.'

'No, sir,' you say truthfully.

'Good. Now, you'll be working chiefly as a cleaner and scullery-maid, under the direction of Molly, our cook. If you're a hard worker and an obedient girl, you won't have any trouble. However, I must warn you' – he pauses and clears his throat – 'the natives in our parts are fearsome. Absolutely deadly with a spear.'

He sees the stricken look on your face and reassures you: 'It's nothing we can't handle, of course – just a little conflict from time to time, that's all. However, you must never leave the grounds unaccompanied, or it will be the last thing you do. Understand?'

'Yes, sir,' you manage to squeak. You've heard of these people, who lived here before the English came. You try to imagine what they might be like. All you heard on the boat coming over was that they have dark skin and live in the bush all over the colonies. You spend the next few hours watching for any glimpses of running figures or flashes of a spear

between the trees. *Calm down*, you tell yourself. *The master said I'll be all right if I don't go wandering off into their lands.*

When you arrive two days later, you discover that the house in Bothwell is newly built, of sandstone mined from the local quarry. It's grand, and the newly-cleared green fields around it give you a feeling of hope – but it's so isolated. Hobart Town seemed small and quiet compared to London, but on your long journey here you noticed there were very few houses or even passing vehicles.

The two other convicts working for Mr Tilsome – Molly the cook and Joe the farmhand – are kind enough but older than you, and they don't tolerate any slackness, putting you to work straight away. Sadly, the master doesn't have a horse – just an ox to pull the cart and the plough – and you don't get to work outside often. You have a small bedroom to yourself in the attic, but most of your waking hours are spent in the laundry outhouse or the kitchen.

The master is a single man, though he has guests around often and works hard on the couple of fields of wheat that he farms. He hopes to one day establish Bothwell as a business-town between north and south, where travellers may buy their wares.

At first you spend every waking minute thinking about Sarah, or your voyage and the foal's birth, or your da. At first, even the earth itself won't stand still: for the first week, your bed at night seems to roll underneath you as if you are still at sea. The air smells strange out here, the sky is a bright, wild blue, and the grass is yellow. No kangaroos have come up to greet you carrying flowers, but you have seen some raucous birds feeding on seed-pods in the tangled trees, flashing like liquid rainbows through the sky.

As time goes by, these things become familiar, but although you now feel more settled here, you're still lonely. One day, you realise that weeks have gone by where the only words spoken to you have been orders.

That very afternoon, the master announces a plan to take the ox-and-cart into Hobart Town the next day. Molly is to go with the master, to stock up on supplies not available in Bothwell, such as sugar, tobacco, candles and cloth. But not an hour later, Molly twists her ankle.

'I think I'll still be able to manage the journey, if I bring you along to help,' Molly says to Joe in the kitchen.

Your mouth opens and words burst out: 'Oh, please, ma'am, can I come to Hobart Town with you instead? I'd be such a help! I'm very strong, and Joe will be needed in the fields here – won't you, Joe?'

Molly raises an eyebrow and snorts. 'You're fair keen, aren't you, girl? Planning to slip off and escape, are you?'

'Have a heart, Molly,' chides Joe. 'It's a lonely life out here for a young lass. I suspect she just wants to see some other folk besides our own crusty selves for a change. Am I right?'

You nod gratefully.

The master consents, though Molly seems irritated by it, and three days later here you are, ready for an adventure in Hobart Town.

The master goes to a meeting in another part of town, and you trail along the bustling waterfront markets in Molly's wake, your eyes as wide as two coins. Some of the buildings are quite grand here, even if it is far smaller than London, and the wharves are full of traffic and the clatter of hooves.

You see all types of people – convicts, sailors, well-dressed gentlemen and ladies. To your surprise, you even see someone who you think might be a native as you walk through the market. He is

wearing a cap and a tatty overcoat, and he is sitting against the sandstone wall of a grand building. This man does not look dangerous to you at all – he just looks like someone who's down on his luck. You give him a little smile as you pass by.

You scan every face you pass, but you don't see Sarah, or – even more unlikely – Da.

A boy in a cap shouts, '*Hobart Town Gazette* – read the latest shipping news!' and you turn to stare. You've just had an idea.

'So you can read, can you?' Molly says and snorts, knowing full well that no girl of your position can. You didn't learn enough letters on the ship to be able to read more than a few words, let alone a newspaper. 'What's of interest to an Irish girl in the *Gazette*, anyway?'

'My da,' you say. 'He may have been transported here too. Perhaps I can find out if he was on any of the ships that have come in just now.'

Molly may seem prickly, but she has a kind heart. 'Not much chance of finding him in the *Gazette*, love – they only report the fancy bigwigs who disembark. The police office has the records of every convict to have set foot in Van Diemen's Land, though – a clerk there could tell you.'

Your heart rises. 'Can we go there now?' you ask eagerly.

Molly snorts again. It seems her sympathy only goes so far. 'You'd have to pay a clerk to read the list to you, and I doubt you have two brass pennies to rub together,' she says. 'Anyway, we're not to waste the master's time with personal errands for missing fathers – I need you at the markets now. Come along.'

As you trail Molly through the markets, a basket of apples over your arm, you can't get the idea of your da out of your head. Molly's right, you don't have two brass pennies to rub together, but you have something much better than that: your golden bracelet, which has been with you through so much, and is even now jiggling lightly inside your petticoat hem.

You could make it seem as if you've just lost Molly in the crowd – slow as she is with her stick, you could get away from her easily – and then run and get the list read. Imagine knowing that your da were here in Van Diemen's Land!

Then you hear a sensible voice in your head: *Imagine giving up your precious bracelet, only to find Da's not even here. He could be dead, or in*

one of the other colonies, or back on a hulk. Then you'd have lost your treasure for nothing. Not to mention that they don't take kindly to runaway convicts here. You could be put back in gaol, or even hanged!

You smile ruefully – that's Sarah's voice you're hearing.

Still, you've survived this far. The sea breeze whips your skirts and hair. Maybe it's time to throw caution to the wind.

✦ To run away from Molly and find out if Da's on the police office list, go to page 139.

✦ To stay with Molly and try to find Da later, go to page 145.

Molly is shuffling further away with her stick, her back turned to you. You're not due to meet the master for another two hours. You might never have a better chance to get away and search for Da.

I have to do it, you think. *I'm going to do it.*

The wharves are bustling, but the crowd is not so dense that you can simply disappear into it. You need a place to hide.

There is an ox-and-cart left unattended only a stone's throw away, with a canvas cover over the cart. Quick as a cat, you dive into the empty cart beneath the canvas, peeking out through a little gap. Just in time! Molly turns around, and realises you are missing.

You had planned to come back to her after you'd had the shipping master's list read, full of apologies and excuses, hoping she would believe that you'd become accidentally separated from her.

Now you hear her words from the other day ringing in your mind: *You're fair keen, aren't you, girl? Planning to slip off and escape, are you?*

Molly is suspicious – much more suspicious than you want her to be: she gives an exasperated groan, rolls her eyes, and begins pacing back towards you, her eyes now narrowed, muttering, 'Knew it was a bad idea...me so slow, and her so fast... "I'll help you," she says. Not likely! Can't trust those Irish girls.'

You stay flat and low beneath the canvas. There is a musty potato smell, and the cart beneath you is splintery. You chance a glance out every so often, and Molly is always still within sight, pacing and cursing.

Then you feel a jolt and a lurch: your cart is moving! Great – it is carrying you out of sight of Molly!

But it is also taking you in the wrong direction, away from the police office, towards God knows where. You'll have to jump out. Already you've reached the end of the wharf area, and now the cart is picking up some speed. Molly is about four hundred yards away. You'll have to jump now!

You roll back the cover and spring to the ground.

Crack! You land on an uneven cobblestone, and your leg buckles under you. You fall heavily sideways and your head hits the stony ground. You cry out, feeling blood trickle down your face. The pain in your foot is breathtaking. You look down, and it looks like a clay foot on a broken doll that has been stuck back on at the wrong angle. Vomit rises in your throat. You try desperately to crawl to the side of the road for some cover before Molly sees you.

Too late! You hear her shout, and see her wave her stick, and a horrible, slow-motion cat-and-mouse chase is on: Molly hobbling along with her stick and twisted ankle; you on all fours, with your badly broken foot and blood dripping into your eyes. Rage chasing desperation.

A nearby shopkeeper realises what's going on and collars you firmly. As he waits for Molly to catch up, he shakes his head.

'*Tsk tsk*. They give you too many chances, you convicts. Your parents' generation would've hanged for half the things you all do — but, no, the judge gives you the chance of a new start. And do you take it? Do you work for your ticket of leave, and make an honest future for yourselves? No! You cheat and swindle and escape and murder. Bloody fools, the lot of you. It's in your blood, no doubt. You should all be hanged.'

YOU ARE NOT hanged, but you are sentenced to a gaol term in the same dim, freezing cells you were held in when you first arrived.

They search you so thoroughly when you arrive that the bracelet in the hem of your petticoat is found. The wardens won't believe it isn't stolen, and it is taken from you. 'Thief' is added to your list of crimes.

Your hair is hacked off, leaving only prickly clumps behind. You are put to work, washing and wringing sheets.

You weakly force yourself through each day, collapsing into a short, dreamless sleep each night. Although a doctor comes to treat your ankle, it never heals. It looks bruised and odd, and after months, your walk forms into a twisted hobble.

The other women call you Hop-Along, but you can't laugh. You can't make yourself care about anything anymore – all feeling has been burnt out of you, leaving ashes. There are no mirrors here, but

sometimes you see your dead-eyed, crooked form looking back at you from a puddle, and you don't recognise it.

When a bout of pneumonia strikes the prison in wintertime, you have no strength to fight it. Day after day, as you force yourself to work, you feel the coughing and the fever dragging you deeper, chewing you, until you think: *Just let it end...I've had enough...*

You begin to hear voices, and in your feverish haze, you're not sure if it's the women in your cell speaking, or the voices of the dead.

'If you had your life over again, what would you do differently?'

'Ah, there's no point in regrets! What's done is done – you can't change the past.'

'It doesn't do good to dwell on it, I suppose. But I can't help thinking, if the timing had been different...if the choices had been different...would I be with him now? Or would I always end up here?'

You don't have the clarity of mind to work anything out. Fever burns through your brain. You think of how drained your ma looked before she died, and you know you're ready to go and join her.

You hope that wherever she is will be a better place than here.

Your cough rattles the last of the strength from your body. You've fought for so long that it will be a relief to stop. You welcome death's quietness, its release. The fever can move on through the gaol, like the hungry fire that it is, looking for more fuel. The voices fade as your breath slows, then ceases.

✦ To return to your last choice and try again, go to page 138.

Once again, I've made the sensible choice, you think a few hours later, rolling your eyes to yourself as you climb up onto the ox-and-cart behind Molly and the master for the long, bum-numbing trip home to Bothwell.

You're glad not to have parted ways with your bracelet, though. You like to think that it wants to stay with you – as if it has a mind or spirit of its own. You suppose it's become something of a good-luck charm to you – if you can call a dead mother, a gaol term, and exile to the furthest-flung place in the world 'good luck'.

You've had some strange dreams about the bracelet since you arrived at Bothwell. You've dreamt you're walking away from the house, wearing only your nightie, following the sound of singing: a woman's voice, in a strange tongue – a keening, bubbly string of words.

In the dream, you are holding your bracelet in your hand, but the colours of the stones are rubbing off on your palm, marking your skin with rainbow

streaks. You want to find this singing woman, and show it to her. You think she'll be able to explain it somehow. But you wander, and wander, and wander, never getting any closer to the source of the singing. Then you wake up.

THE MORNING AFTER your arrival home from your trip to town, you are in the kitchen, peeling potatoes, your head crammed full of thoughts. A fresh breeze wafts into the room, tempting you outside. You haven't been able to stop thinking about Da.

There's only a slim chance that Da has been transported to Van Diemen's Land, and yet having the list read at the police office is the only chance you have of finding out for sure.

You are trying to think up a plan of how you'll achieve that on your next trip to town...and feeling frustrated with yourself that you didn't take your chance yesterday...and wishing you were outside...and thinking of that strange dream you had again last night...and in the end, your head gets so full that it forgets where your fingers are, and you slip and slice yourself with the peeling knife.

'Damn this!' you say, and you plonk down the slightly bloodied potato and storm outside to take a breath. Molly and Joe are nowhere in sight, and the master is away at another meeting in Bothwell town.

Bruno, the dog, darts past your legs. He is wagging his tail as if he's running to greet an old friend, but he just ducks under the gate and runs off to an empty stand of trees. At least, you thought they were empty, until you see a dark hand emerge to scratch behind Bruno's ears, and a head of curly black hair duck down to greet him.

You don't know whose grin is wider – Bruno's or the boy's.

There is a native boy just outside the back gate, and yet you can't bring yourself to feel frightened of him – not when you see him with Bruno, so playful and relaxed. Still, you slip back inside the door, and watch through a crack.

The boy, wearing an animal-skin skirt and no shirt, strolls into your garden as if he owns the place. Which, it occurs to you, he probably *did*, before the master came along – just as you Irish owned your country before the British took that too.

Bruno trots alongside the boy adoringly. With just one finger, the boy lifts the latch on your chicken coop. It swings open, and he ducks inside. You are incredulous: that door *always* gets stuck and creaks. He did this so easily that it's clear he's been here before. Then out he pops, curly hair bobbing under the doorframe, a black-and-white chicken under one arm. He gives Bruno another pat, and then, *swish*, silently closes the creaky coop door and—

Hang on, you think. *Am I just going to let this boy waltz out of here with one of my chickens?*

All right, they're the master's chickens. But there's precious little food around here, apart from what you grow yourselves. You need that chicken!

You burst out of the door, and the boy turns, astonished. There is no spear in his hand, but you do see a little knife swinging from a string around his waist. The chicken clucks under his arm, pressed against his bare torso. The boy seems younger than you – maybe ten or eleven.

For a long moment, you size each other up. There's no sound but Bruno's gentle panting. Your eyes are locked.

Then, suddenly, there are footsteps and a voice from the kitchen – Molly is back. The boy turns and runs out the back gate in a flash.

You hesitate. Should you give chase, get back your chicken, and win praise from Molly and the master? You don't enjoy being stolen from.

Mind you, since becoming a convict, you have plenty of sympathy for people caught stealing. Is one less chicken so terrible? You could let the boy go, and speak to Joe later about putting a lock on the coop – although somehow you doubt that would stop this clever, agile-fingered boy.

✷ If you give chase to the boy and your chicken, go to page 150.
✷ If you let the boy escape and go back inside, go to page 156.
✷ To read a fact file on Tasmanian Aboriginal people, turn to page 261, then return to this page to make your choice.

'Hey,' you shout, 'that's my chicken!'

You sprint through the trees, following the glimpse of the curly-haired boy's back. Your legs carry you like the wind, over spiky grass tufts, up a hill of those strange pale-limbed trees with the dark, waxy leaves. You can hear insects chirping, your breath coming in gasps, your blood pounding.

You've just lost sight of the boy when you hear a chicken squawk. You hurl yourself towards the sound, determined he won't get away.

You smell the smoke too late, and almost run into the fire. You pull yourself up short, arms windmilling.

There is a woman sitting beside the fire. She is completely naked except for a grey fur necklace, and she is wringing the chicken's neck.

The woman sees you and stands up warily, tossing the chicken onto the coals. The air fills with the horrid stench of burning feathers. You back away, your breath coming in short gasps.

The young, curly-haired boy steps out from the

bush, places a hand on the woman's arm as if to protect her, and draws his knife. He calls one word in his language and, silent as smoke, three men appear through the trees. They all have skin as black as the night. One wears his hair in muddy ropes. Another has a spear, which he is raising, pointing straight at you.

You run – run like you've never run before, certain that at any moment now, you will hear a *swish* as the spear flies through the air, and feel the agony as it pierces your back. Your feet seem to hardly touch the ground. You hear people pursuing you, their footsteps pounding the ground not far behind.

Is this how I die? you think. *Is this finally it?*

Not today. Not if you can help it. Your breath gushes in and out, in and out, in time with your legs, forming a fast, steady rhythm.

I have to live – find Da, I have to live – find Da, I have to live, your mind chants, in time with your breath.

You look over your shoulder, your arms and legs still pumping forward, and see that you're still being followed. And then it happens. The ground is suddenly not there. You see the edge of the cliff as you are running over it.

Your arms flail in empty air. The moment of flight stretches out, so that it seems to happen very slowly, as if you are dreaming. How strange to be dropping, somersaulting down, your body plummeting, all sight and sound a blur.

You hit the bottom of the quarry with a crack like a gun going off. The breath is snapped from your chest and you are gulping like a fish, trying to force the air back in, but your chest has closed tight and you can't breathe.

Finally, though, the air starts to enter your chest again, a little at a time, and it comes out in screams of pain. Your thigh bone has snapped, and the pain is excruciating. The pain is so big that it swallows up the rest of the world, swallows up all thought, and squeezes you in its fist. You pass out.

WHEN YOU NEXT open your eyes, you are still in the sandstone quarry, but now you are surrounded by the people who were pursuing you. The man who had the spear is lifting a big rock above your head. He says something in a firm tone. His eyes are grim.

You brace yourself for the rock to land on your head – the final blow that will end your suffering

and your life. But the man with the muddy hair reaches out and stops him. They argue.

You manage to look down. Your skirt and petticoat has been ripped away, to reveal an open wound: a fragment of broken bone sticks out of your thigh, blood pulsing out around it. The blood feels warm and sticky. A wave of pain lifts you like a boat. You close your eyes.

YOU OPEN YOUR eyes. You smell roasting chicken, and your stomach rumbles. Maybe there will be some left from the master's dinner and you'll share it with Molly.

But all you can see are pink clouds, and then a concerned strange face. You realise there are hands on you: hands pressing your thigh; hands holding you down. You writhe in pain. Hands grip your ankle, and there is a flurry of talking, a very strong pull, and then...relief. Your thigh still hurts, but the agony is gone.

You lift your head a little to see your helpers tying your ankle firmly to a branch splinted down the side of your leg. Your skirt and petticoat have been mostly ripped away. What's left is red with blood.

The blood is still rising and draining from your thigh, unstoppable as a spring. Someone takes a blood-soaked pad of bark from the wound and presses down a new one, to try to stem the flow. You feel overwhelmed by dizziness. You close your eyes.

YOU ARE HAVING that same dream you've had since you arrived here: the woman's voice singing, in lilting, knotted strands of voice, worn with time. You go to follow the song, then realise it's right around you. You have found the song. In your dream, you look down at the bracelet in your palm, and it's whole again.

YOU OPEN YOUR eyes. There are stars above you. You can hear a quiet breeze in the leaves. Someone is pushing warm chicken meat between your lips. As you chew, they also let a little water dribble from their cupped hands into your parched throat.

You try to reach down to your petticoat hem, although your petticoat is not there anymore, of course. You want to hold your bracelet, as you did in the dream. It's agony to try to move.

A warm, grandmotherly face appears above you. She pats your arms and holds your hand.

'I have a gift for you,' you whisper. 'A bracelet in my petticoat – I want you to have it. Please.'

She strokes your hair gently back from your face and begins to sing the song from your dream. There are tears in her eyes.

Everything blurs, as though the scene were an ink picture with water tipped over it. You feel a creeping coldness, despite the fire, the meat and the song.

'You tried to save me,' you whisper. 'Thank you.'

You don't know if the old woman understands your words, but both of you understand that life is spilling from you steadily, running out. Broken bones can heal, but too much blood has flowed out of the wound, and there's not enough left to keep you alive.

All pain falls away, and it's just you, the old woman, the song and the stars. You close your eyes.

✴ To return to your last choice and try again, go to page 149.

You duck back into the kitchen. You notice that your hands are trembling slightly.

Molly is looking at the bloody potato and the peeling knife. 'Did you do yourself an injury?' she asks.

'Oh... yes,' you say absentmindedly. You'd forgotten about your cut.

'You look like you've seen a ghost, lass. Surely a little cut's not upset you that much?'

'Oh, it's not that,' you say. 'I just saw—'

The words catch in your throat. Molly ploughs on busily, without noticing.

'The master has invited Mr and Mrs Wright and Mr Jenkins for dinner tonight – important guests apparently. I'll need you to fetch two chickens and have Joe wring their necks so we can get to plucking them straight away,' she orders.

You gulp. There were six chickens to begin with. Two will be dead for tonight's dinner, and another was just spirited away by the curly-haired boy.

Do you need to tell Molly what you just saw?

Pretty soon, people will be asking why there are three chickens left, instead of four. Not to mention that the fat hen the boy took was a good egg-layer.

You don't want to admit to Molly that you witnessed a crime and then let the culprit get away with your best chicken. And there's more... you remember the boy's dimples, his young, brown eyes locked on to yours, and you admit to yourself that you don't want to get him in trouble, either.

You'll have to make up a story – maybe a tiger took it! You've heard of these striped, dog-like beasts that roam Van Diemen's Land, though you've never seen one, and you're not sure a tiger *would* steal just one chicken and then disappear without a trace.

You curse yourself. If you lie to protect a native boy, a thief, you'll wind up in trouble again. It's better that Molly knows what really happened – she can't blame you for not tackling a stranger who was armed with a knife. If you tell her truthfully what happened, the missing chicken can't possibly be blamed on you. You can't afford to lose your position at this house. You really should tell Molly.

Tell her, go on, you urge yourself. *Come* on *now, you foolish, stubborn...*

But something in you just doesn't want to.

Molly is staring at you, one eyebrow cocked. She has noticed that you're behaving strangely. 'What are you muttering about?' she asks sharply.

✦ If you tell Molly that the boy stole the chicken, go to page 159.
✦ If you cover up for the boy, go to page 166.

You force the truth out in uncomfortable shoves.

'One of our chickens was stolen – the fat black-and-white one. A native boy did it. I would have run after him... but he had a knife.'

Molly is upon you immediately in a whirlwind of sympathy.

'A native! Dear God, no wonder you look pale! Oh, you're shaking! Didn't I tell you not to go out? Good grief, his whole family has probably surrounded us. Chickens – next they'll be having sheep, and then they'll kill every one of us, too. Why not!'

Molly, usually so bossy and practical, is in a right lather. You want to tell her to stop being hysterical – there was absolutely nothing frightening about the boy, or the native man you saw at the market in Hobart Town either. But then you remember the master's words to you on your first journey out to Bothwell: *You must never leave the grounds unaccompanied, or it will be the last thing you do.*

Suddenly Molly gasps. 'Joe! He's out there cutting firewood! *Joe!* At least he has the axe,' she says desperately, 'if they don't spear him from behind. *Jooooe!*' she hollers out the doorway, flushing crimson, turning back and forth like she doesn't know what to do with herself.

It's as if you've told her there is an army of ogres charging over the hill wielding clubs and spears – not that a bare-chested boy with dimples and a hen under his arm was here and has since run away.

Joe appears in the doorway, looking sweaty and perplexed. 'You ladies all right in here?' he asks.

Molly flings herself on him like a tightly coiled spring.

She's sweet for him! you realise in wonderment, watching a blush rise to Joe's sweaty brow and hearing the tears catch in Molly's throat.

'Natives!' she blurts. 'Did you see them, Joe?'

'Not a thing,' he admits. 'They're quiet, though – famous for being quiet as they move. We should tell the master. What did they take?'

'A chicken!'

'Just one chicken?'

'That's just the start! Don't you shrug at me! They'll be *back*, and next time—'

'I'm not shrugging. I just thought from the noise you were making...'

Molly is livid now. She marches out of the room.

Joe looks at you helplessly and scratches his head. 'Guess I'll go and chop some more wood, then,' he says and ambles off.

YOU'RE NOT SURE what Molly told the master, but by dinnertime it's clear that he takes the same fearful view of things as she does. You hear him say as much as you serve the roast chickens that night.

'We must teach them a lesson,' the master is saying, and Mr Jenkins nods firmly, while Mrs Wright looks terrified and Mr Wright pats her hand and puffs out his chest like a protective rooster.

The skin on the back of your neck prickles horribly. *What does he mean by that?*

'They'll know who's in charge around here once I've introduced them to my musket,' Mr Jenkins says grandly. 'It's the latest model from Britain. It arrived just last week. Fires like a dream – *crack!*' he cries.

You realise that you've stopped your serving. Dread curdles in your stomach. *He can't be serious?*

But Mr Jenkins just chuckles, and Mr Wright does more hand-patting, for Mrs Wright has jumped at the sudden sound of his shout.

YOU LIE AWAKE in bed that night, hearing echoes of the men's boastful voices in your mind, as proud as boys pretending to be kings. *Introduce them to my musket. Teach them a lesson.* You toss and turn, the dread in your stomach growing into a storm.

As you left the room after dinner, you heard the master say: 'Before dawn tomorrow – agreed?' and the murmur of the other two men's assenting voices.

Oh God, you pray, *what have I unleashed? Please stop it, please.*

You dream of men on horses. Screams. Running through the bush. Your bracelet lost and broken underfoot. Men with growling mouths full of dog's teeth. A chicken with a broken neck. Blood. Silence, but for your heart pounding.

YOU HEAR SOUNDS of the master and his two friends leaving on horseback before dawn. Molly acts righteous and self-satisfied all day long, while you are unable to keep your mind on your daily chores.

When the master finally returns late in the afternoon, you and Molly are given the task of scrubbing his clothes.

There is sweat and dirt on his shirt, as you expected, but then you see the patches of blood, slowly turning the soap froth a pale-pink. Your own blood runs cold.

The drumming of the clothes being kneaded back and forth across the washing board is the only sound between you and Molly for a long time.

Eventually she says: 'I thought he'd frighten them off...that's all.'

You struggle to find your voice. Is this the boy's blood in your washing water? His mother's?

'He was only a boy, Molly,' you mutter in a choked voice. 'It was only a chicken.'

Molly shakes her head, as if trying to erase a horrible picture. 'That's how it starts,' she says grimly. 'Just one chicken, and then before you know it...No. It's for the best, what the master did. He did it to protect us.'

You drop the damp clothes into the bucket and race outside, your fists clenched. The only noises in

the garden are the bird calls, but in your mind, you can hear pounding hooves, gunshots and screaming. Vomit is rising in your throat, but you swallow to force it back down. You fiercely wipe the pink suds from your hands on your apron, as hot tears run down your cheeks.

A FEW DAYS pass in stony silence. Then, just as things start to feel more normal again, the boy's family comes.

They don't come charging over the hills with clubs and spears – they come quietly, like Joe said. It's before dawn when they surround the house – the best time to attack.

Your attic bedroom window shatters. A burning branch lands on your bed. The curtains go up in flames. You peer out and see the warriors outside through the heat haze, rippling like light on water, a circle of spears and eyes.

There is the noise of more windows breaking. Burning branches light the house from every direction. You hear screaming, and doors banging, as Molly, Joe and the master run from room to room in a panic, finding no way out of the circle of flame. The flinging doors fan the flames, until the place is an inferno. Your door is closed, and you are too terrified to leave your room.

Your bed is ablaze. You try to smother the flames with your spare dress, but it isn't working. Smoke is pouring under your door. You're fighting to breathe.

Through the shattered window, you see Joe, running from the house yelling, with an axe in his hand. He is felled by a spear before he has taken three steps.

That's how it starts, you hear echoing woozily through your mind, as you cough wretchedly from the smoke and drop to your knees. *Just a chicken*.

And this is also how it ends: a chain of theft and retribution. Everything is a chain – a circle. A circle of warriors, drawing tighter around the house. A knotted rope of song. A noose; a leg-iron; a shining bracelet. Circles that wind around you, binding you to this moment. Repeating circles, which you didn't break, which will now, finally, break you.

THE END

✦ To return to your last choice and try again, go to page 158.

You feel the palms of your hands grow clammy. You wipe them down on your apron.

'Nothing,' you lie to Molly. 'I'm not muttering about anything.'

'Well, go out and get me those chickens, then. Get a move on!'

Why did I just do that? you ask yourself. *Lie to protect a stranger – and a thief, at that.*

You sigh. You know from the look on his face and from the playful pats he gave Bruno that he meant no harm.

Your whole life has been battered and twisted and shaped by punishments for things you've done where you've certainly meant no harm to anyone. As has your da's life. You can't damage a young boy's life and family just for that – you can't encourage this unfairness to continue. You just want things to be simple.

You go to get a chicken, and when you come back into the kitchen, a rusty-red beauty under your arm, you say: 'It looks as though one of the chickens is missing. Perhaps it was a tiger. I've overheard the master say they're a menace around here.'

Molly furrows her brow, too busy to question you, and seems to accept the lie.

But the next week, the curly-haired boy is back again. Again, he waits until Molly and Joe are not around. Again, Bruno grins delightedly as the boy enters the coop and comes out holding one of your last three chickens.

'Hey! You're not having that one too!' you shout through the kitchen window, and without even thinking, you rush out there and snatch the hen from his arms.

This takes the boy so much by surprise that he just stands there watching as you put the hen back in its coop and shake your finger at him like your ma always did to you when she was cross.

He grins and shakes his finger back at you, teasing you.

You'll be able to tell if a person's all right or not by looking in their eyes, your granny used to say. This boy has friendly eyes. He looks right into your face for a while, and there's a playful challenge there. Then he seems to get embarrassed and looks away.

Bruno rolls joyfully at the boy's feet. 'That's

Bruno the dog,' you tell him. There is a long pause, where he looks at you curiously. You try again. 'What's "dog" in your language?'

He looks puzzled. 'Breunoth erdog.'

'That's a funny word for a dog. Say it again? Breu... what?'

'Breunoth erdog,' he says, pointing at Bruno.

You try to repeat it, feeling baffled. 'Breu... breunoth... erd – *dog!*' You suddenly realise your mistake and burst out laughing. 'You're saying "Bruno the dog"!'

The boy joins in with your laughter. Soon you are both shouting, 'Brunothedog! *Brunothedog!*' and Bruno is leaping around you, yelping with excitement. You laugh until you have to wipe away tears.

YOU DON'T SEE the boy every day after that, but you always hope that you will. You learn that his name is Waylitja, and that this is also the name of a type of bright-green bird that looks like a small parrot.

When you have time to be together – when the others are not nearby – he points out the noisy green birds as they fly overhead, or brings you a gift of homemade string, and you show him soap bubbles, and how the buckle on a belt works.

Sometimes he speaks his language, and you love the way it sounds. You wonder if you could learn it.

In the olden days, you know that all the Irish people spoke Gaelic, before the English came with their language and their guns. *There are whole worlds inside our language*, your granny would tell you, and then she'd sing a song in Gaelic that you can't quite remember now.

There must be whole worlds in Waylitja's language too. You wonder about all the things he knows.

Your fourteenth birthday comes and goes. No one knows or cares. You wonder where Sarah is now, and imagine all the food you'd eat together for your perfect birthday meal. You only wish you could find out something more about Da – that would be the best present. You still haven't managed to get back to Hobart Town, let alone find a way to have the police office list read.

Spring turns to summer. It has been one year since your ma died, and you miss her dreadfully. The lonely days continue to drag by, summer ticking away, until the weather cools and the leaves on the little oak saplings in the garden begin to change. The big tangled trees beyond the garden seem to stay dark-green all year round, like pines. You can't help but stare off at those trees when you're supposed to be working, looking for Waylitja – the only person in your whole far-flung world who smiles at you, who wants to spend time with you. You want him to know how grateful you are, just for that.

But the next time he visits, Waylitja is quiet, and there's something heavy and sad behind his eyes. He says something in his language. He is touching his chest and gesturing away.

You take his hand. 'What's the matter?' you ask him. 'Are you all right?'

He sighs deeply and takes his hand back. He's staring over the horizon and then back to you. Imploring you with his eyes to understand.

Waylitja reaches into a bag that hangs from his waist and brings out a glistening handful of shells. He gently places them in your hands. They are beautiful – each one is no larger than a baby's fingernail. Some of them are little peachy-pink cones, some are as round and white as tiny pearls, and the prettiest ones of all glisten with all the colours of the rainbow. They remind you of the first stone on your bracelet.

You shift your hands and realise that the shells are strung together, into two necklaces. They are so finely clustered, you can't even imagine how much time it would have taken to make them.

How could anyone make a hole in each fragile little shell like this without crushing it? you wonder, and you lift your head to ask Waylitja, but he is gone. There is simply a space where he used to be – as if you've dreamt him and then woken up.

You feel grief wash over you. Somehow, you suspect these necklaces are a parting gift. Again, you wonder about all the things Waylitja knows: the mysteries of the land that is his home.

YOU THINK OF Waylitja every time a green parrot flies overhead. You wait days, weeks, then months, for him to reappear, but he never does. Meanwhile, in your friendless world, you have nothing to do but think and work and sleep, and think and wake and accept orders and work again.

By the time winter has settled in, you decide Waylitja is not coming back, and you reach a

decision. You will take one of his necklaces to Hobart Town at the next opportunity, and use it as payment to have the list of convicts in the colony read. You will be so sad to part with one of your beautiful necklaces, but you think Waylitja would understand. You hope and pray that it will bring you a step closer to finding Da. Now there is nothing left to do but wait...

✦ To read a fact file on what happened to Waylitja's people, turn to page 263, then return to this page.
✦ To continue with the story, go to page 173.

One frosty winter's morning, the master calls you, Molly and Joe into the drawing room to speak with you formally.

'As I am now well-established as a merchant here in Bothwell, and the home and grounds are now of a sufficiently comfortable state, I have sent for my wife and child to join me. They will be arriving three months hence.'

You try not to let the shock show on your face. You've been working here nearly a year and you always thought the master was single!

Won't it be grand to have a child join the house, you think. *We could do with some noise and laughter round here.*

'I'll be taking another servant into my employ,' the master continues stiffly. 'So I'll be travelling for Hobart Town in the morning, to choose a suitable woman.'

'I'll come with you!' you blurt, then silently curse yourself – it's awfully bad manners to interrupt the master, especially since you neither asked permission nor spoke politely.

Molly looks furious, the master merely shocked. Joe is stifling a chuckle.

But luck is on your side: the master agrees to allow you to travel with him and Molly, and this time you beg Molly beforehand to find time in the day for you both to make a trip to the shipping master's office, and she begrudgingly consents. She has seen how hard you've worked and how patient you've been.

When Molly asks what you plan on paying the police office clerk with, you decide to show her Waylitja's necklace, but knowing how scared she is of natives, you say you found it near the edge of the garden.

'Who'd have known they could make something pretty like that,' she says. 'Still, I doubt the clerk will take it as payment.'

YOU WEAR YOUR petticoat with the bracelet in the hem on the journey to Hobart Town, just in case. You take one of the necklaces with you, leaving the other hung on the mirror in your bedroom, a keepsake of Waylitja.

To your astonishment, in town, when the

shipping clerk shakes his head at the necklace and prepares to turn away, Molly steps forward in your defence.

'No other natives in the world make necklaces as fine or as pretty as these – any sailor would buy them from you to sell at his next port. They're right valuable – two shillings a piece in Victoria, I'm told. And this girl's a fine worker and a lovely lass. She only wants the chance to see her poor father again. Have a heart, won't you?'

You feel yourself blushing in surprise and joy.

The minutes tick by in the stale office, as the clerk reads the disembarkation list for the last year and eight months, as it was near that long ago now that you saw Da being sentenced, and he could have arrived any time since then.

You are doing what Ma used to call 'bargain-praying', which she'd warned you the Lord didn't always like, but nonetheless you are promising Him your devotion and spotless behaviour for the rest of your days if only you can find Da when the clerk says: 'Patrick Ryan – Patrick Sean Ryan? He's here,' and jabs his finger at the page.

Your heart leaps out of your chest like a dolphin out of the water.

'Well, he was here in November last year, anyhow,' continues the clerk. 'As a convict aboard the ship *Midas*, which sailed from London, and arrived 23rd November 1825 with your da on board. There's nothing noted of where he went to from there. Says he has a fourteen-year sentence, so hopefully he's behaving himself and working for a ticket of leave.'

When you step out of the office, you take Molly's hand and dance a little jig. She shakes you off, embarrassed but pleased.

'You're mad as a lamb in the springtime,' she says.

You start singing, 'My da is in Van Diemen's Land, oh blessed be the day!' to the tune of 'Beautiful Eileen' – and you don't care who hears it.

'Thank you, Waylitja,' you whisper, with a smile as big as a rainbow. You see a green bird flash overhead and feel tears prick your eyes.

YOUR SECOND GREAT shock for the day comes soon after.

You and Molly meet up with the master at the wharf and accompany him to the same gaol you were held in when you first arrived in Hobart Town. Your master is looking over a line of wretched,

downcast women, aiming to choose his next servant, when you suddenly see that one of them is Sarah.

You gasp, and almost fall to your knees. Tears spring to your eyes.

'Sarah!' you hiss. 'Sarah, it's me!'

She looks up, and her eyes grow wide. The state she's in makes your stomach drop. Her lovely thick hair has been shorn off, leaving raggedy patches behind, and her brown eyes have sunk into her face, which is no longer round but gaunt. Her eyes are surrounded by a bruised darkness, and her prison smock shows her painfully thin wrists and ankles.

It takes every ounce of your self-control not to throw yourself at her. *Carefully, now*, you think. *Play this right, and she's ours to take home...then we'll live together like sisters, as I promised her.*

'Pardon me, sir,' you whisper, tugging at your master's elbow. 'If it interests you to know, I can personally vouch for the good character of one of these women here.'

It's not much, for one convict to vouch for another's good character, but as the master has nothing else to go on, he looks slightly interested. 'Which one?'

'Her, sir. Sarah MacBride.'

Sarah raises her head in acknowledgement and then looks respectfully back at her toes.

'She's an honest, loyal worker,' you go on. 'A sensible and good girl.'

The gaoler overhears you. 'MacBride is not a sensible or good girl,' he sneers, loudly enough for everyone to hear. 'She had a second chance at life after murdering her own father with a broken bottle...and she ran away from her new master as soon as she had the chance. She's not fit to wipe your boots on, sir. She'll corrupt your servant-girl, there' – he nods at you – 'and you'll never see either of them again.'

Sarah's voice comes out in a sob. 'I was ill-used by them!' she chokes. 'My da and Mr Taversham both. Every day!'

'Shut *up*!' shouts the gaoler, and tears begin running down your face. To see Sarah again, and think you might not be able to save her, or hold her...it's almost unbearable.

To your amazement, though, the master speaks directly to Sarah. 'Who did you say he was – your old employer?' he asks.

'Mr Taversham,' she whispers, 'in Jericho.'

You can hardly believe it. Sarah was in the settlement right next to Bothwell the whole time!

'I know the man,' your master says, with a disgusted tone to his voice that you've never heard before. 'He's a drunkard and a womaniser. *He's* the one not fit to wipe my boots on.' He turns to the gaoler and says: 'I'll be informing the Police Magistrate that Taversham's not fit to be assigned any more female convicts. Sarah MacBride, you can come with us.'

✦ To read a fact file on convicts in Van Diemen's Land, turn to page 269, then return to this page.
✦ To continue with the story, go to page 180.

Why did the master take Sarah home with you that day? Was it to get back at the man he so disapproved of, Mr Taversham? Did he feel sorry for her? Or was it that he trusted your judgement of her character? You and Sarah have time to talk about this, and a million other things, curled up in the attic bedroom you now share. She's your sister and best friend rolled into one. You never get sick of each other's jokes, and you seem to know just what she's going to say before she says it. She makes the work lighter and your life in the household so much happier.

Three months pass swiftly. You turn fifteen, and Sarah bakes you a special cake. Mrs Tilsome and Robert, the master's wife and six-year-old son, arrive at the end of spring.

Mrs Tilsome is quiet at first – seeming a bit stunned to be in Van Diemen's Land, perhaps – but slowly she begins to settle in, and she always speaks kindly to you, Sarah and the other staff.

Robert – whose nickname is Bobby – is a whirlwind.

You wonder sometimes why you ever looked forward to having a child in the house! There is always extra mud on the floor, or something he's broken needing repair. Still, he certainly brings the house to life.

Summer arrives, and the household celebrates Christmas and New Year. Not long afterwards, the master plans another trip to Hobart Town, and agrees to take Bobby along to see the sights, if you and Sarah will come along to supervise him. Molly and Mrs Tilsome seem pleased to have the chance to get things done around the house in Bothwell while Bobby's away.

Now you stand in the sunshine at the far end of the wharves, watching Bobby play happily on the rocks. 'Don't get your shoes wet!' you call. Bobby just laughs.

Sarah has gone off to a disreputable part of town known as Wapping, looking for the next clue to your da's whereabouts…

'Mr Taversham was a horrid old drunk, and a heavy gambler to boot,' she told you when she first arrived in Bothwell, 'and he'd entertain all sorts – travellers and vagabonds. Some of them were scary and you'd hope never to see them again, but one of them, Mike, came often, and he knows things. He helps moving livestock from the wharves all over

the colony, so he sees all sorts go by. Now that you know your da *did* arrive here, and when, perhaps Mike can help us to find him. And...and...he is a very sweet man, too.'

You caught her blushing then, and gasped. 'You have a beau!' you squealed. 'Have you kissed him? Sarah, tell the truth – is this a plan to find my da, or to meet up with Mike again?'

'Both,' she admitted, the pink in her cheeks spreading to her ears, 'and no, of course I didn't kiss him! It was too risky – you know we can get sent back to gaol for things like that. But maybe one day...' She sighs.

That conversation was so long ago now. You're so excited to have this opportunity to visit Hobart Town again today, and investigate. You wonder how Sarah is going on her hunt for Mike. You hope for her sake that he's as kind and true a man as she thinks he is. Despite having gone through so much, Sarah has not lost her hopeful habit of seeing only the best in people.

Just then, you feel an odd prickling on your neck and turn to see a man watching you. He is young, and handsome in a quirky way – he has a long nose, ginger hair flopping to one side of his brow, and pale-blue eyes. His head is tilted to one side, his eyes resting on your face intently, a bemused half smile playing about his lips. He's wearing a brown jacket, a high collar and braces, and leather boots.

After regarding the man for a moment, you look away, feeling a little fluttery. But when you turn back, he's still standing there, seemingly transfixed by you. You look into each other's eyes again, for what seems like the longest time. You know the ladylike thing to do would be to turn your back and ignore him, but you find that you can't. He fills you with a curiosity to know him better.

A wail from Bobby snaps you to attention. He is lying sideways on a rock, clutching his knee. His little face is screwed up tearfully. You leap across the rocks to get to him. The ginger-haired gentleman is suddenly at your side. You sit Bobby up and dust him down. His knee is bleeding a little.

'Allow me,' says the gentleman. His voice is rounded, well-educated, but with a deep, lush Irish accent. It's wonderful to hear a voice so instantly evocative of home. He ties his handkerchief around Bobby's knee, pats his head, and turns to go.

'Wait!' you cry. 'Why were you staring at me just now?'

He pauses to reply, but just at that moment you hear Sarah's voice echo across the rocks as she returns, waving.

'My apologies,' the gentleman says, smiling. 'You just remind me...of a very impressive man I know. You could be his daughter, the likeness is so striking.'

Your heart starts to pound. 'Who?' you ask, with bated breath.

But the mysterious gentleman sees Sarah approaching and says hurriedly, 'I've said enough. I really must be off. Good luck,' and he strides away over the rocks towards town at a pace you'll never catch with Bobby in tow.

'Your da was at Macquarie Harbour!' Sarah cries breathlessly, joyfully, as she reaches you. Your heart is still pounding.

'Sarah, that's no cause for celebration,' you say, stunned. On a place called Sarah Island in Macquarie Harbour, on the wild, isolated west coast of Van Diemen's Land, is a fearsome gaol. Hobart Town may feel like exile to some, but Macquarie Harbour is exile even from here: the lowest rung of Hell itself.

'He tried to run away from a work gang here, and was sent to Macquarie Harbour – but it's rumoured he escaped!' she pants. 'Mike had a friend who

knew all about it. You do know what your da was taken away for in the first place, don't you? That he was a freedom fighter in the Irish rebellion, who set fire to a government vessel?'

You nod, wondering who on earth she found in Wapping who knows so much about your da. 'But no man can truly escape from that place,' you whisper. 'Sarah, he'll have starved to death in the wilderness.'

'Not all of the escapees starve!' she cries. Then she sees your face, and stops. 'I'm sorry. I was so happy at having found all this out that I forgot how worried you'd be. Your da must be a very strong man. Mike's friend seemed sure that if anyone could make it, he would.'

Bobby sniffles and lets out a little moan. He unwraps the hanky from his knee to more closely inspect the damage. You'd forgotten he was even there for a moment.

All of a sudden, you see that the handkerchief is embroidered with three initials: LSO. Could the 'very impressive man' that gentleman claimed you so resemble possibly, just *possibly*, be Da?

You feel like you are right on the brink of finding some answers, but that you just don't have enough information yet. Now the sun is sinking lower, and

you and Sarah must take Bobby to meet Mr Tilsome and begin the long journey home – right away, in fact, or you'll be late. But you know that, once you've returned, you'll be stuck in Bothwell for many months before another trip to Hobart Town takes place.

You are itching to leave Sarah to return home with Bobby, while you run away to follow one of these new leads – either chasing up Mike's friend in Wapping, or searching for the mysterious gentleman you met at the rocks.

But if you run away, you'd be committing a crime. If you were caught, you'd be imprisoned again, for who knows how long. What's more, you would lose your chance of a ticket of leave. It would mean another indefinitely long absence from Sarah, and an uncertain future.

You feel torn in three different directions.

---

* To go to Wapping and search for Mike's friend, go to page 187.
* To follow the mysterious gentleman, Mr LSO, go to page 193.
* To return to the master and look for your da again next time you're in town, go to page 197.

'Sarah,' you say urgently, leaning close and looking into her brown eyes, 'who did you meet in Wapping who knows my da?'

She shrugs, looking confused. 'His name was Connor Murphy. He's a friend of Mike's – well, Mike knows him, at least – and—'

You break away from her and start to jump over the rocks. You want to say goodbye, but Sarah is so sensible that she'd stop you from going.

'What the blazes are you doing?' she shouts, 'You'll make us all late for the master!'

'Don't wait for me!' you call back. 'Tell him I got lost... or kidnapped. Yes, that's better!'

'No man would be fool enough to kidnap some mad bloody Irish girl with about as much discipline as a wild monkey!' she hollers back. 'You'll lose the lot – no ticket of leave, no job. For God's sake, *stop!*'

You throw a glance over your shoulder. Bobby's little jaw is about hanging down to his knees with all the yelling and cussing flying back and forth

between the two of you. Sarah is tugging him over the rocks as fast as he can go, but he's still teary from his cut knee, and she can't keep up with you – nor will she ever desert Bobby.

She's too good, you think. *So dutiful she won't even take a chance when she gets one.*

You know that's not a fair thing to think, but you are trying to block all doubts from your mind. Sarah is shouting out everything she can think of: 'For the sake of your poor mother! For the sake of our friendship! Damn it, stop and think it through!' She keeps yelling until you clamber up onto the docks and disappear into the crowd.

You make your way around the docks in a big crescent to your right, until you reach Wapping. The place is a maze of shanty-houses and muddy tracks built around the Hobart Rivulet, which is not much more than an open sewer at this point in its journey to the sea. The place is thick with workers from the wharves: you pass a tavern, and a man pushing a stinking cart piled high with dead seals.

You're nervous, and it must show on your face, because the people on the streets look you up and down with hungry curiosity. Some give black-toothed chuckles and point.

A drunken voice shouts, 'Connor, you're a bloody mug!' and you turn to see a man throwing a punch at another man, who ducks and spills his beer on himself then launches himself at the first man. Next thing, they have both thrown themselves against the nearest wall in a heap, laughing and swearing.

'Ah, but I'm the best bloody mug in the business, and you know it!'

You step up to them, nervously. 'Is your name Connor?'

He snorts. 'You can hear all right then, as Marshall's been shouting it all over Wapping!'

'Connor Murphy?'

His eyes narrow. 'What's it to you?'

'You know my da, Patrick Ryan. I want to find him.'

Connor snorts again. 'Sarah's been talking to you, I suppose. I don't know anything more than what I told her: your da's somewhere in the bush east of Macquarie Harbour, either alive or a pile of bones, the devil knows which. You'll find him when he wants to be found, as has always been the way with Ryan. Now bugger off.'

The other bloke, Marshall, interrupts. 'Now don't

be rude, Connor. I'm sure there are many more tales you could tell about this little lady's da if we get some rum into you…'

YOU AGREE TO join Connor and Marshall in a pub down a dark alleyway, where they buy each other moonshine rum.

'I saw your da wrestle a thylacine to the ground once,' Connor claims. 'He wears its teeth in a necklace…

'Even the redcoats fear him. He can throw a cannonball fifty yards…

'I saw him take three men out with one punch…'

The evening grows deeper and the stories wilder. You aren't sure you believe anything Connor says, but you can't bring yourself to interrupt him, or stop yourself from listening, either.

You try a sip of the rum yourself and the liquor strips your throat with flame.

'He picked the lock on his cell door using a nail from his boot…' Connor claims.

'Women faint with adoration when he passes by…'

'He can travel like the wind, silent as a

blackfellow or raging like a storm, whichever suits his purpose...'

'He's so strong that other men drink their whiskey with one of his beard hairs in it as a concoction to give them almighty strength.'

Connor slaps his knee. Marshall throws his stinky arm around you.

'And oh, how he loves his daughter. If he has one weak spot, you're it. You're the last name on his lips in prayer under every starry night. He's sworn an oath to save you, and by God he'll keep it.'

At that point in the story, Marshall leans over you and tries to plant a hairy, slobbery kiss on your lips. You scream and duck. He lunges for you and knocks over the wooden table, and glass shatters everywhere.

Connor starts swinging at Marshall, yelling, 'She's young enough to be your daughter, Marshall. Ryan'll bloody scalp you. Didn't you hear a word I said?'

Marshall shouts in reply: 'He's dead. Ryan's dead for sure. You're mad to think otherwise!'

Before you can help yourself, you've joined in the fray, kicking Marshall and spitting like a cat, so blinded by emotion that you don't notice the soldier

coming up behind you until his hand falls heavily on your shoulder. You are taken away.

YOU ARE SENT to prison, charged with disorderly conduct and escaping your master. Every new day that you awaken within those stone walls feels like a bad dream. Only a few months ago you rescued Sarah from here. Now you have fallen lower than low, your hair roughly shorn from your head as punishment, blisters on your hands from the long days of scrubbing laundry in the burning sun.

Hope feels like some scarce, long-forgotten luxury – like butter, or a fur-collared cloak. No one will ever come to rescue you as you rescued Sarah. Or so you think.

✦ In this matter you have no choice. Go to page 226.

'Sarah,' you say, gripping her hands urgently, 'take Bobby back to the master. I'm not coming home with you.'

Sarah laughs and shakes her head. 'Oh, very funny, wild Irish girl.'

'Sarah, I love you dearly, and we'll be together again someday, but I have a chance to find my da *right now* – the best chance I've had! A gentleman came while you were away; he said I reminded him of someone. See this hanky? LSO – they're his initials. I'm sure he knows Da!'

Sarah looks gobsmacked. She is still shaking her head, but she isn't laughing anymore. Bobby tugs at her hand. 'Sarah? My knee's all right now. Let's go and meet Father.'

Sarah's gaze hardens. 'Yes, we *all* will,' she says firmly, 'and no more nonsense from anyone.' She looks at you pointedly, and reaches out to take your wrist, as if you were another child.

You wrest your arm away. 'He's my flesh and blood, and he's somewhere right here on this island.

If I give up and go back to work now, I'll go mad!'

'I think you already have,' she says quietly. 'I thought I was a sister to you.'

Tears spring to your eyes. You'd rather she yelled and cursed – you can't bear the sight of her so disappointed, so crushed. After all she's done to help you today, you are treating her like this...

You shake your head and push the feelings away. You don't trust yourself to speak, so you just blow her a kiss, then turn and run. Your stomach twists itself into knots, and the lump in your throat grows. But you climb up onto the docks and start running up the hill towards the shops in town, the direction in which the mysterious gentleman went – and, just like that, you are gone. You are now an escaped convict on the run.

You slow down to a walk so that you don't look suspicious. You know Sarah won't call the redcoats on you, but you do wonder what lie she'll tell the master. And what will Bobby say?

You look down at the hanky in your hand, spotted with Bobby's blood. 'L' could be for Leonard, Louis, Liam, Lawrence...

You reach the main street, but the mysterious gentleman is nowhere to be seen. You start to feel

like the world's biggest fool for taking such a risk. Where will you stay tonight? How on earth will you hide and survive? Sarah's right – you're mad.

Taking a deep breath, you open the door of the nearest grocer's shop. 'Excuse me, ma'am,' you say to the woman behind the counter, 'a gentleman dropped this – I'm looking to return it to him. A tall Irish gentleman with ginger hair.'

The woman looks you up and down suspiciously. 'How did you know he was Irish?'

You pause, gulp. 'I…overheard him talking. His initials are LSO – see?'

'Yes, I see. Had a bleeding nose, did he, this Irishman? Can't say as I know anyone of those initials. Plenty of Irish names beginning with "O", though – O'Grady, O'Brien, O'Malley, they're all "O"-somethings, aren't they? Well, leave it here. I'll put it up on the noticeboard there, and someone might claim it.'

'If you don't mind, ma'am, I'd rather take it to the gentleman in person…'

'Well, it so happens I *do* mind. Either you don't trust me to take care of a bleeding hanky for a while, or you think there'll be some sort of reward for you if you deliver it yourself. Either way, I don't want you in my shop! I suppose your accomplice is around the shelves nicking something while you distract me with a cock-and-bull story, is that it? Out – go on – out!'

You begin to rush out of her shop just as a red-coated soldier steps in. The sight of his uniform, the gun slung over his shoulder, the commanding way he is staring at you, triggers some sort of rabbit reflex in your brain, and for a moment you stare at him, stock-still. Then you bolt.

'After her!' shouts the shop owner, based on nothing but her suspicion and her prejudice against Irish people, convicts, or both.

You realise as the soldier's hand grabs your shoulder that you shouldn't have run. It made you look guilty – which you are: guilty of escaping your master, abandoning your job, and forsaking your dear friend Sarah ... although they don't include that last bit in your sentence.

Soon, you find yourself behind the very same stone walls of the gaol that you rescued her from. And no one is coming to rescue you. Or so you think.

✳ In this matter you have no choice. Go to page 226.

You think of what a risk Sarah took for you today, going to Wapping to search for clues, despite it being such a dangerous area. Now that you have some leads on Da, the best thing to do is to wait patiently for a chance to use them.

You pick Bobby up off the rocks. 'Let's go,' you say, wishing there was another way. But you've learned that to keep working, keep surviving, and be sensible is the only way to get by in Van Diemen's Land.

You spend the whole trip home wishing you could turn back to Hobart Town and search for more clues, but only a week later, the answers come to you.

It is a hot January day. You are hanging out the washing when you hear a rustle in the trees. You hope that it's Waylitja... but there's no one there.

Soon afterwards, you are emptying the kitchen scraps onto the compost heap when you think you see a shadow flash by. Suddenly, your arms are pinned to your side, and a strong hand is clasped firmly over your mouth. You feel the barrel of a gun pushed into your back.

'Pardon me, madam,' says a smooth voice in your ear, 'but your homestead is being, as they say, "bushranged", by the Shadow Gang. Lead me to the master of the house.'

Stumbling, you lead the man inside. The kitchen is empty, but a second bushranger comes inside shortly thereafter with Joe in a headlock, followed by four more men. You manage to twist a little in the bushranger's grip, and catch a glimpse of a red handkerchief tied over his face.

The bushrangers fan out through the house then, searching for other occupants. You are separated from Joe, prodded along by your captor, another two of the bushrangers following you, down the corridor off the kitchen, and then up the stairs towards the drawing room...where you know Sarah is serving Mr Tilsome and his guest, Mr Reid. You're so glad that Mrs Tilsome and Bobby are out of the house running errands.

The bushrangers can hear voices murmuring from the drawing room. They follow the sound. Sarah squeals and drops a teacup as they enter the room, and the two men jump to their feet.

'Please be seated, sirs,' says one of the bushrangers. He has a clear, strong Irish voice and he wears a black patch over one eye. 'We are the Shadow Gang. We do not kill unprovoked, but if any of you dares challenge us, we will not hesitate in feeding your guts to the dogs.'

The master and Mr Reid retake their seats, ashen-faced.

'Thank you,' says the bushranger.

Soon you, Sarah and Molly and Joe, who have been brought into the drawing room too, are all on the floor, bound together with rope, guarded at gunpoint by two men. The master and Mr Reid are bound into their chairs.

Some of the other bushrangers are circling the room, filling hessian sacks with anything valuable they find: a crystal liquor bottle, an oil painting, a lace cloth.

'Our captain would like a chat with you,' announces one of the men guarding you, and a giant of a man strides into the drawing room.

He wears a dirty white shirt and leather waistcoat, and he has also tied a black handkerchief over his face, so that only his light-blue eyes and fierce eyebrows are showing. His hands look strong enough to break a boulder and are laced with white scars. His footsteps make the teacups rattle in their saucers. All the bushrangers salute.

The giant stops. He's looking at you. Those blue eyes. You know them. The realisation hits you like a tidal wave, and you struggle to breathe – it's Da.

The silent air seems to crackle. Everyone is waiting for the bushranger captain to speak, but he seems momentarily dumbstruck. Then he wrests his eyes away from you and clears his throat. 'I am Captain Shadow, Commander of the Shadow Gang.'

His voice throws you back in time: you can hear him on the streets outside of Newgate, fighting to get to you. *To hell with you and your chains.*

His voice has grown huskier but tougher, and it is deep with defiance. 'I take no orders,' he continues, 'and I live outside the law. This colony is founded on theft and injustice. The Shadow Gang does not wish to spill your blood. We simply wish to live as free men.'

Captain Shadow – Da – orders one of his men to bring the master's rum and tobacco, to share among the servants. The master, tied to his chair, is glaring so hard it looks as though his eyebrows might catch fire with outrage. Then Da kneels in front of Molly and Joe in turn, to light a pipe or offer a glass of liquor.

Da kneels in front of you. You try to swallow the lump in your throat and feel one hot tear run down

your cheek. His voice comes softly, muffled under the handkerchief, so quiet that only you and Sarah hear what he says next. His huge hand is shaking as it touches yours.

'Don't say a word, my darling.'

'Please,' you whisper urgently, 'take me with you!'

'You don't want this life,' he mutters. 'Trust me. Work until your sentence is done, and I promise I'll see you again.'

'But Da—'

'Not another word,' he says softly. 'You don't know me.'

Your heart is burning and fizzing like water on a hot pan. You can see the sense in what Da's saying – if you go with him, you would become an outlaw; if you stay and work, you'll earn legitimate freedom. But can you really take the chance of never seeing him again?

'Who are you?' the master asks. 'I demand to know your true identity!'

'Who is Captain Shadow?' Da chuckles. 'Oh, all the redcoats with their nooses and guns would love to know too, as would the journalists, and the Governor himself. I'm a dead man. I'm a free man. That is all you need to know.'

You suddenly realise that you know how you can

force Da to take you with him – by threatening, here and now in front of everybody, to reveal his true identity!

It would be an irreversible choice. This life would be over, and you would live the rest of your life in defiance of the system, always fighting to stay one step ahead of the hangman's noose.

Or you can say nothing, and have the life you planned: a ticket of leave, and eventually a house, job and family of your own choosing.

Will you threaten to reveal the identity of Captain Shadow and force Da to kidnap you?

✦ If you threaten to reveal Da's identity so that you can join the Shadow Gang, go to page 203.

✦ If you keep working towards your ticket of leave and let Da go for now, go to page 213.

✦ To read a fact file on Matthew Brady, a real-life Tasmanian bushranger who escaped from Macquarie Harbour, turn to page 271, then return to this page to make your choice.

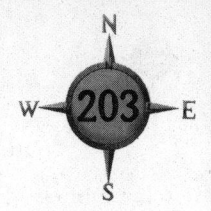

You take a deep breath, and say loudly from the floor, 'I know who you are, Captain Shadow.'

Sarah gasps and wriggles next to you. Your da whirls on his heel. The other bushrangers raise their guns and take aim at you. The master looks gobsmacked.

'Take me with you, or I'll reveal who you are right now,' you demand. You hear the click of muskets preparing to shoot.

'Hold your fire!' orders your da.

The other bushrangers glance at each other, bewildered.

'It's a rough life,' says Da, his blue eyes steadily meeting yours. 'Not one I'd wish for anyone's daughter.'

Da doesn't want to reveal his relationship to you, as it would give away his identity, but you know he's warning you of the hardships to come.

'It's what I want,' you say clearly. 'To hell with them and their chains.'

Your da sighs audibly, but his blue eyes crinkle with his proud Irish grin. 'We're taking your servant-girl,' he announces to the master as he unties you from the others and hauls you to your feet. 'And I'll wager she's braver, faster and smarter than the whole Shadow Gang combined. So if any of you mugs think you can track her down, that'll be the last thought ever to pass through your mind. If you're quiet, the Shadow Gang takes only your gold – but speak of this to anyone, and we return to take your life.'

You leave the house, and it feels like you're stepping out from under a heavy shell you've been made to carry. You hitch up your weighty skirts, and your petticoat with the bracelet still sewn into its hem, and you swing your legs over the hot, dusty flanks of Da's horse.

Oh, the feeling of a horse cantering beneath you! It's as if, since you arrived in Van Diemen's Land, you've been living a half life – an obedient, paper-cut-out life – but now, riding with Da's arm around you, your heart floods, your body comes back to life, and you remember. You remember the fresh fields of Ireland, the flowers, your sister, and the songs your granny used to sing. You can't help but sing one aloud as you ride:

'Oh, the girl, she was brave, and bright as the sun...

'...and none who tried could catch her.

'For her heart, it was filled with the song that it sung...

'...of freedom, freedom forever.'

DA'S CAMP IS deep in the bush, three hours' ride from Bothwell. Your bed will be a hessian sack stuffed with grass; your bath, the cold stream; and your only friends for now, Da and the six bushrangers in his gang.

You wish you could have brought Sarah with you, but you don't know if she'd like this tough life, and you know that eventually – in eight more years, when she's eligible – she will gain her ticket of leave and marry her beau Mike from Wapping. You hope that she will be happy. She certainly deserves to be.

Da's horse comes to a halt, and he swings you down from the saddle. 'This is it, at least for the next few days until we move on,' he says, as he leads you

through the trees towards some canvas tents and a circle of rocks, where one of the bushrangers has begun to light a fire. 'Home of the Shadow Gang.'

✦ To continue with the story, go to page 207.

Da sits you down by the fire and introduces you to the bushranging gang. They seem delighted to learn that you are their captain's long-lost daughter.

'This boy here is Jimmy McMahon,' says Da, gesturing. The bushranger sitting nearest you tugs down his red handkerchief to reveal a boyish face barely old enough for shaving, framed by a shock of raven-black hair. 'Jimmy's a wiry little runt, but he can run like the wind. We call him Dash.

'This here's Stephen Everett, or Wombat, as he's known. What he doesn't know about survival in the bush isn't worth knowing. We owe our escape from Macquarie Harbour to him – and of course to Lewis "One-Shot" Fletcher here, who needs only one shot to kill an animal from any distance. He's a finer marksman than any soldier in the King's service.

'John Williams here – Inky is his nickname – is a mighty clever forger, of bank notes, certificates and the like. He also has a great mind for strategy; he's smarter than a fox, and more wily to boot.

'Now who've I missed? Oh, Samuel and Sean O'Grady, brothers and Irish nationalists like myself. Sam has a talent for fixing and making things – boots, saddles, traps and the like – so we call him Useful. As for his brother here, old one-eye...'

Da nods to a bushranger seated across the fire from you, Sean, who looks just like his brother, Sam, except that he wears a patch over one eye. He was the one, you remember, who threatened to feed Mr Tilsome's guts to the dogs.

'They call me Useless,' Sean interjects, and all the men start chuckling. 'I lost my eye when another prisoner in Macquarie Harbour attacked me with a burning stick. It's true I'm not much help practically, but—'

'But we keep him round because he sings like an angel,' interrupts Inky. 'Go on, Useless, show the lass what you can do.'

Sean closes his one eye and begins to sing. In that moment, even the earth stops spinning, and the rocks stop growing moss: the whole universe pauses to listen. How can a one-eyed bushranger have a voice so pure? How can a man who's travelled through Hell sing like Heaven?

When he stops, the only sounds are the occasional

pop of the campfire and a snuffle from your da as he wipes away a tear.

'Now you see,' says Da after he's collected himself, 'there'd be no point in fighting to be free if we didn't have Useless here to remind us what freedom sounds like.'

'So...' muses Wombat, who is stout and bristly like his name. 'What can *you* do, girl?'

There is an expectant pause round the campfire. Da is waiting to hear from you too – he wants you to stand up for yourself.

You think back over the journey you've been on: you've been reunited with Da; you saved Sarah from the prison; you made friends with Waylitja; you helped a foal to be born in a storm; you crossed the world; you survived Newgate Prison and stood up to Nell; you lived by your wits on the streets of London when it seemed not a soul in the world cared whether you lived or died; and the whole adventure began when you calmed a panicked horse. Or perhaps the adventure began before then – perhaps it began when you were only a small child, and your da taught you the meaning of freedom.

'What can I do?' you ask. 'I can protect my friends, and keep my promises to them. I can survive when

the sky is black and my family is dead and lost to me. I can cross the world on a prison ship. I can find new life where death and violence abound. I decide how I live. My choices are my freedom.'

Suddenly, you know what the lady who gave you the bracelet meant. When she gave you the bracelet, she gave you options. It was up to you to decide what to do with it: she was giving you freedom. Freedom to choose. That's what the bracelet means.

You take a knife and run it through the stitches on your petticoat. You remember making these stitches two years ago; they have not been broken, and neither has your promise to keep it safe.

When you understand its meaning, you'll know it's time to pass it on.

The seven gemstones of your bracelet tumble into your palm. After all this time in your hem, the links between the stones on the bracelet have bent and opened; the chain is now broken into seven separate gems.

Seven gems, and seven men in the Shadow Gang...it seems right, somehow. You give your favourite gemstone, the glistening rainbow stone, to your da. Inky the forger gets the stone that's dark-red like the ink or wax seals he can forge, and the brothers Sam and Sean (you refuse to call them Useful and Useless) get the two matching bright-green stones.

You pause to think, then you give Dash the stone that's black as his hair. One-Shot gets the clear, star-white stone, just as he always takes a clear shot; and Wombat, who knows the ways of the bush, gets the dark-forest-green gem.

'Mine's a fire opal,' says Da. 'Williams, that's a ruby.'

Da inspects all the stones and names them: there's a fire opal, a ruby, two emeralds, a diamond, an onyx, and the dark-green malachite.

Although you were never schooled properly in reading and writing, thanks to your lessons during the voyage to Van Diemen's Land, as you think about the names of the gems, and the sounds of the letters, a puzzle starts to come together in your mind...

F for fire opal, R for ruby, EE for the two emeralds...then diamond, onyx and malachite...

'It spells freedom!' you exclaim.

'SO IT DOES,' breathes Sean in wonder.

'How about that, then,' mutters Wombat.

'For as long as we keep these stones,' announces Da, 'may we ride free together, united against all of those who would take our freedom away.'

You know that life from here on will be tough. You may end up with your neck in the hangman's noose. You may get sick of life on the saddle and in the scrub. You may end up shooting a soldier, or being shot.

But your grassy bed, Da's warm, strong hand on your back, the snuffling horses, the wheeling stars, and Sean's sweet songs by the crackling campfire are all you need right now.

Oh, the girl, she was brave, and bright as the sun…

…and none who tried could catch her.

For her heart, it was filled with the song that it sung…

…of freedom, freedom forever.

THE END

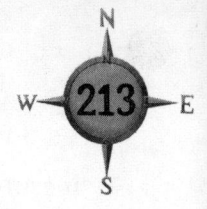

You resolve to keep quiet, for Da's safety and your own, but you watch him closely as he moves about the room, drinking in these moments in his presence.

You notice he has a limp now, and wonder if he gained it on the treacherous escape from Macquarie Harbour; and you notice the horse-and-smoke smell of him, something you've loved since childhood. You catch a glimpse of his beard under the edges of the handkerchief and notice there's some grey mixed into the auburn.

The great Captain Shadow does not speak often – just to give orders to his gang while they comb the house for valuables. It seems he doesn't trust himself to look at you, either, lest his emotions give him away. Yet, just before he and his men leave, he speaks to the master and you can hear the deep flood of longing in his voice, resonating like water under rock.

'Sir, am I right in thinking you have a wife and a child? If so, you'll know that whatever we take from

you today, you remain free to keep your greatest treasure. If only I could steal my own family back from death and from servitude. This gold and silver I've taken from you today is simply our way of making a living – but they were my life. Cherish your family, and treat your servants well, otherwise the Shadow Gang will return. If you force us to come a second time, it will be not to take your trinkets, but your life.' With that, he unties the master and Mr Reid from their chairs and leaves the room.

You hear the bushrangers galloping away. The lump in your throat subsides, but your whole body feels wobbly and weak.

Mr Tilsome and Mr Reid untie you, Sarah, Molly and Joe. You swear there's a puzzled, wary look in Mr Tilsome's eye when he looks at you and says: 'You'd all best take the rest of the afternoon off, I think. In honour of the oddly poetic Captain Shadow.'

THE SUMMER ROLLS on. The air smells of dry grass, and Molly turns to making salads and cold cuts instead of stews and roasts.

One day, a boy from Bothwell, Reggie Martin,

son of the postmaster, comes to the house and calls over the back-garden fence: 'I have a letter here, for a Miss Ryan!'

You are shocked! It's the first letter you've ever received. 'Whoever is it from, Reggie?'

'I'm sorry but I'm not sure, miss. My father asked me to deliver it.'

You can't read well; you remember learning your alphabet on the boat, but you never went to school. But Sarah was schooled until she was eight or nine years old, and she manages to read it to you. It's sealed with wax, and the ink on the page is curly and blue, like lichen.

Dear Miss Ryan,

Please excuse my boldness in sending you this letter. The moment I saw you on the rocks in Hobart Town, I was struck not only by your beauty, but by your resemblance to a great hero of mine. This man is my hero not only due to his bravery and love of Ireland, but because of a promise he made to his daughter: a promise to cherish and protect her, to the ends of the earth.

I believe you know the man of whom I speak. Please be assured that he is, for now, safe, and

carrying on his usual business. I am in touch with him from time to time.

It my greatest wish that you would be kind enough to meet with me. I would be honoured if there is any way that I may uphold my hero's promise to his daughter, whom I believe to be a young woman with a courageous spirit and an extraordinary mind.

With the greatest respect,
Lachlan Seamus O'Riordan

You think of the handkerchief, still spotted with Bobby's blood, in the corner of a drawer in your bedroom... of the young, ginger-haired gentleman who couldn't look away from you that afternoon on the rocks.

'LSO,' you whisper to Sarah. 'Lachlan Seamus O'Riordan.'

A WEEK AFTER you send your reply, Lachlan arrives at the homestead, introduces himself to the master as a travelling merchant, and then asks for the use of one of his servants that day to wash and fold some large samples of cloth that were damaged

when his cart ran off the road on the way to Launceston.

'The cloth's just fine,' murmurs Lachlan in your ear as you ride away together, and he pats the large bundle of fine cloth in the back of his cart. 'On loan from a friend in Hobart Town. I'll give one of the pieces to Mr Tilsome as a gift, to thank him for giving me some time in your company, if it pleases you.'

'Yes, sir,' you whisper. You wish your knees would stop shaking.

'Oh, please,' begs Lachlan, 'I am not "sir" to you. In fact, *I* take orders from *you*, for your father is the most respected Irish nationalist in Van Diemen's Land – not to mention being the infamous Captain Shadow!'

You laugh, but at the same time feel tears prick at your eyes. 'I saw him. He robbed us! I only wish we could have had a conversation... that I could see him again.'

'That's what he said too,' says Lachlan. 'I told him I'd do anything to make it happen – especially if it meant I was able to meet you again. Climb down here and follow me, but be quick – he only has a moment. It's risky for him, coming back this close to town only a month after the robbery.'

Your heart is pounding in your ears. Long grass crackles under your feet, and you see a small green parrot swoop through the trees in front of you and think of Waylitja.

Lachlan steps on a stick, which cracks and makes you jump. He takes your hand, then leads you down into a stony gully. You hear footsteps approaching from behind a tree, and then there, standing in front of you, is Da.

You fling yourself into his arms, and his hug is so tight that it compresses all the breath out of you. It feels so good to be squeezed by your da – so secure that there's nothing to do but surrender to his bigness and strength. It's like being a child again.

He lets you go, and air rushes back into your lungs. He shakes Lachlan's hand heartily, and says: 'Thank you. From the bottom of my heart. This means the world to me.'

'To both of us,' you add.

'Oh, when I saw you in that house in Bothwell, I thought my heart was going to burst,' Da says, cupping your chin in his hands. 'I've been searching for you ever since I came to Van Diemen's Land – and now look at you, you're as beautiful as your mother was when I first met her.'

Da pauses, and wipes away a tear. You stare at each other's faces in mesmerised silence. You feel like you're in a wonderful dream that you don't want to wake from. Your da takes you by the shoulder and guides you through the trees.

'We've got so many stories to share,' he says huskily. 'But come, make yourself comfortable and meet the rest of the Shadow Gang, now they're not busy robbing Mr Tilsome's house!'

Da leads you behind the tree, to a campsite with a fire, with six men sitting around it.

✦ To continue with the story, go to page 220.

Da sits you down by the fire and introduces you to the bushranging gang. They seem delighted to learn that you are their captain's long-lost daughter.

'This boy here is Jimmy McMahon,' says Da, gesturing. The bushranger sitting nearest you tugs down his red handkerchief to reveal a boyish face barely old enough for shaving, framed by a shock of raven-black hair. 'Jimmy's a wiry little runt, but he can run like the wind. We call him Dash.

'This here's Stephen Everett, or Wombat, as he's known. What he doesn't know about survival in the bush isn't worth knowing. We owe our escape from Macquarie Harbour to him – and of course to Lewis "One-Shot" Fletcher here, who needs only one shot to kill an animal from any distance. He's a finer marksman than any soldier in the King's service.

'John Williams here – Inky is his nickname – is a mighty clever forger, of bank notes, certificates and the like. He also has a great mind for strategy; he's smarter than a fox, and more wily to boot.

'Now who've I missed? Oh, Samuel and Sean O'Grady, brothers and Irish nationalists like myself. Sam has a talent for fixing and making things – boots, saddles, traps and the like – so we call him Useful. As for his brother here, old one-eye…'

Da nods to a bushranger seated across the fire from you, Sean, who looks just like his brother, Sam, except that he wears a patch over one eye. He was the one, you remember, who threatened to feed Mr Tilsome's guts to the dogs.

'They call me Useless,' Sean interjects, and all the men start chuckling. 'I lost my eye when another prisoner in Macquarie Harbour attacked me with a burning stick. It's true I'm not much help practically, but—'

'But we keep him round because he sings like an angel,' interrupts Inky. 'Go on, Useless, show the lass what you can do.'

Sean closes his one eye and begins to sing. In that moment, even the earth stops spinning, and the rocks stop growing moss: the whole universe pauses to listen. How can a one-eyed bushranger have a voice so pure? How can a man who's travelled through Hell sing like Heaven?

When he stops, the only sounds are the occasional

pop of the campfire and a snuffle from your da as he wipes away a tear.

'Now you see,' says Da after he's collected himself, 'there'd be no point in fighting to be free if we didn't have Useless here to remind us what freedom sounds like.'

'So...' muses Wombat, who is stout and bristly like his name. 'What can *you* do, girl?'

There is an expectant pause round the campfire. Da is waiting to hear from you too – he wants you to stand up for yourself.

You think back over the journey you've been on: you've been reunited with Da; you saved Sarah from the prison; you made friends with Waylitja; you helped a foal to be born in a storm; you crossed the world; you survived Newgate Prison and stood up to Nell; you lived by your wits on the streets of London when it seemed not a soul in the world cared whether you lived or died; and the whole adventure began when you calmed a panicked horse. Or perhaps the adventure began before then – perhaps it began when you were only a small child, and your da taught you the meaning of freedom.

'What can I do?' you ask. 'I can protect my friends, and keep my promises to them. I can survive when the sky is black and my family is dead and lost to me. I can cross the world on a prison ship. I can find new life where death and violence abound. I decide how I live. My choices are my freedom.'

Suddenly, you know what the lady who gave you the bracelet meant. When she gave you the bracelet, she gave you options. It was up to you to decide what to do with it: she was giving you freedom. Freedom to choose. That's what the bracelet means.

You take a knife and run it through the stitches on your petticoat. You remember making these stitches two years ago; they have not been broken, and neither has your promise to keep it safe.

When you understand its meaning, you'll know it's time to pass it on.

The seven gemstones of your bracelet tumble into your palm. After all this time in your hem, the links between the stones on the bracelet have bent and opened; the chain is now broken into seven separate gems.

Seven gems, and seven men in the Shadow Gang... it seems right, somehow. You give your favourite gemstone, the glistening rainbow stone, to your da. Inky the forger gets the stone that's dark-red like the ink or wax seals he can forge, and the brothers Sam

and Sean (you refuse to call them Useful and Useless) get the two matching bright-green stones.

You pause to think, then you give Dash the stone that's black as his hair. One-Shot gets the clear, star-white stone, just as he always takes a clear shot; and Wombat, who knows the ways of the bush, gets the dark-forest-green gem.

'Mine's a fire opal,' says Da. 'Williams, that's a ruby.'

Da inspects all the stones and names them: there's a fire opal, a ruby, two emeralds, a diamond, an onyx, and the dark-green malachite.

Although you were never schooled properly in reading and writing, thanks to your lessons during the voyage to Van Diemen's Land, as you think about the names of the gems, and the sounds of the letters, a puzzle starts to come together in your mind...

F for fire opal, R for ruby, EE for the two emeralds...then diamond, onyx and malachite...

'It spells freedom!' you exclaim.

DA NODS IN amazement, and Lachlan murmurs: 'You're extraordinary...I mean, *that's* extraordinary.'

For the next hour, you share stories with your da, of his incredible escape from Macquarie Harbour, and of your voyage to Australia. But all too soon, the sun starts to sink behind the trees, and you have to go. Your da kisses your forehead.

'It may be a long time before we meet again, my dearest,' he says. 'There's a price on my head. Once you have your ticket of leave, I would love to join you, but until then I'll have to lay low.'

Lachlan salutes him. 'Captain Shadow, it has been an honour and a privilege.'

'Look after my daughter, O'Riordan.'

'She's an astonishing person who has endured more than I can imagine. She's far braver and wiser than I,' replies Lachlan. 'But yes, with her permission, I daresay we'll try to look after each other.'

Your heart swells.

'Goodbye, Captain Shadow,' you whisper. 'Stay free.'

You and Lachlan walk back into the bush, arm in arm.

✦ To continue with the story, go to page 249.

A couple of weeks have passed inside the bleak walls of the Hobart Town gaol. All hope that you will ever be free has fast slipped away.

This morning you have been shepherded, along with all the other women, into the courtyard for display. This is what happens when masters come to choose a new convict servant. You don't know how to feel during these sessions. Part of you feels eager to please, desperate to be taken away from the prison, hopeful that you'll be chosen by a master who at least feeds you well and treats you fairly. But part of you feels angry at being so powerless, the way all of you convicts can be pushed around and traded like animals.

From talking to Sarah, you know that you might be taken away by a man who will beat you, and there's nothing you can do about it. Some of the convict women gaze up beseechingly; others stare back at the men with a steady, furious scowl. Most of the women, including you, seem to spend these regular sessions looking mutely at their toes.

'Mister Lachlan Seamus O'Riordan,' the overseer announces to the guard, and a man is ushered into the courtyard.

Your ears prick up at the Irish name. It almost seems like you've heard it before.

Lachlan...Seamus...O'Ri— *Oh! LSO!*

You head snaps up, and there he is: lanky body wrapped in an overcoat, ginger hair falling over his brow, and pale-blue eyes as sweet as the summer's sky.

'I have your handkerchief!' you cry out, before you can stop yourself. The women around you titter as you mumble, 'I mean...they...they took it from me, when I came here.'

You feel as stupid as the time when you were ten that you tripped over carrying a tray of eggs.

'Silence!' snarls the prison guard.

But Mr O'Riordan is looking at you very kindly. 'How could I forget you?' he asks, and there is tenderness in his voice.

The prison guard looks astonished, and a little disgusted. Mr O'Riordan notices, and immediately changes his tone.

'She'll do. Come with me,' he orders with curt authority.

'Polly over there is a much stronger worker, and better behaved by a country mile,' the guard admonishes him.

But Mr O'Riordan is having none of that, and you are out the door, by his side, within minutes.

He leads you to his horse-and-cart, has you sit up beside him rather than on the back, and heads out immediately towards his homestead, which he tells you is at Crayfish Point, where the Derwent River widens and mingles with the sea.

You are so stunned by what's just happened that you can barely utter a word.

Then Mr O'Riordan shocks you further by taking one of your hands in his. 'Now, tell me what I've wondered since I first met you,' he says softly. 'Are you, or are you not, the daughter of Patrick Sean Ryan?'

Your heart is pounding giddily. You take a deep breath and squeeze his hand. 'Yes! He's my da. Tell me everything you know!' You pause, remembering your manners. 'If you please, Mr O'Riordan, sir.'

'Call me Lachlan,' he replies, and the broadest grin you've ever seen almost splits his face in two. 'Well... where do I begin? Your da and I know each

other through the Irish independence movement. He fought bravely in the Irish Rebellion, I'm told – I wasn't born yet back then…'

Lachlan tells you he is nineteen years old, from County Cork, Ireland, and that he and his father came out to Van Diemen's Land of their own free will three years ago, although his father died last year. He's making his living as a farmer, but his secret passion is to assist Irish political prisoners to escape from Van Diemen's Land to freedom. When he found out Da had been transported here, Lachlan tracked him down.

'He was a labourer for a government gang, building bridges, at that time. I promised that, as soon as I could, I'd work out a way to help him escape.

'He urged me to hurry, because he didn't know how much more he could take. He seemed heartily sick of the orders, the work, the oppression by those beastly gaolers and their whips. And he was in such a rush to find you. He'd made a promise to save you, he said. He didn't want to grind himself to the bone in the convict system while there was a chance you were here and alive.

'While I was putting a plan in place to try to

save him, he took matters into his own hands. He attacked his gaolor and tried to escape. But they caught him. He was sent to Macquarie Harbour, a place so fearsome the devil himself knocks before entering – yet once again your da escaped. He's nothing if not a rebel.'

'And then what?'

Lachlan shakes his head. 'I wish I could tell you that he made it out of the fearsome west coast alive. But there's been no further sign of him. He may have headed north along the coast, or over the ranges towards Hobart Town. Still, they haven't caught him. So he may be out there. And there's no fiercer man to take on that adventure than your da. Don't give up hope – I haven't.'

Lachlan's story continues all the way home, then winds its way inside by the fire, where he sits you down in an armchair and brings you crumpets, as if you were a lady and he your servant. It's a wonderful little home that he's built for himself, using timber and clay from the forest all around.

'Thank you,' you say, a little embarrassed. 'I don't know what I've done to deserve such kindness.'

Lachlan sits next to you, and looks into your eyes. 'You deserve every kindness under the sun,' he tells you. 'It's the masters of this brutal colony who don't deserve the luxuries they have. I'm sorry I couldn't get your da away from them sooner.'

'I'd like to help you in your work to free Ireland,' you tell him. 'I'll do whatever it takes.'

Lachlan gives you another of his grins. 'I'll be sure to let you know.'

YOU FALL INTO a homely rhythm of cooking, gardening, and eating meals fit for royalty – roast chicken, and blackberry pie sweetened with honey. It's the first time that Van Diemen's Land has not felt like an exile from home: it feels, for all its thick forest and strange bird calls, a place that could become home.

Your first political act, when it comes a few weeks later, is to travel into Hobart Town alone to pick up a priest's robes from the cleaner's. The robes will be a disguise for an Irish rebel, who is going to attempt to escape from convict labour in Van Diemen's Land to America, where he can live as a free man. It doesn't sound too hard – picking up the robes from the cleaner's, that is. Escaping to America sounds impossible.

At the cleaner's, you hand over the paper token Lachlan gave you and the cleaner nods, goes out the back, and returns with a heavy, soft parcel wrapped in string and brown paper.

You didn't realise a priest's robes would weigh so much. You can't fit the parcel into the satchel you brought, so you hug it to your chest as you walk out of the shop, waiting for a voice to shout: *Hey, you! Stop!*

There is no shout, though; no whistle. You are simply a servant-girl, going about her business.

You are within sight of your horse-and-cart when you stop short. Standing beside the cart, their arms crossed, are Mr Tilsome and a constable in uniform.

Your old master is looking right at you. 'That's the one,' he says to the constable. 'I thought I recognised her.'

Just then, Sarah runs up beside you, gasping for breath. 'Run!' she cries. 'The master's here, and – oh God, he's already seen you!'

She stares at him open-mouthed, realising the trouble she's going to get in for having been seen warning you.

Should you run, or stay and lie to Mr Tilsome and the soldier about what you're doing here?

+ If you run, go to page 234.
+ If you stay where you are and lie, go to page 237.
+ To read a fact file on Irish political prisoners in Van Diemen's Land, turn to page 273, then return to this page to make your choice.

You grab Sarah's hand, tucking the parcel under one arm. Your heart is pounding. There is no time for thought, only flight.

'Run!' you cry, and for once Sarah doesn't tell you to stop and be sensible, because she can see the angry constable closing in, and she knows she's in as much trouble as you are.

Your feet pound the cobblestones. You duck and weave through the crowd. It's hard to run holding hands, so you let go of Sarah.

A whistle is shrieking. You nearly knock down an old lady with a basket as you shove past her. Cries and shouts ripple in the air. A man makes a wild lunge for you, and you swerve. You glance back over your shoulder. Sarah is slowing. The man who missed you is lumbering towards her. She ducks to get out of his way and stumbles towards the edge of the dock, towards the water.

'Sarah!' you scream. She's lost her footing. Like a doll, she tumbles over the edge and into the black water in a wreath of bubbles, her skirt floating and tangling like a jellyfish.

You can't swim, but you don't stop to think about that. You drop your parcel, and launch yourself over the edge of the dock to save her.

Though it's a summer's day, the water is icy, and it squeezes the breath out of your chest as you sink, fighting your way through a mess of rising cloth and bubbles. You can't see Sarah below you until you push your own skirts out of the way.

Your clothes are dragging you down. You fight to quell the panic rising in your chest, and kick to the surface to snatch a mouthful of air before the weight of your skirts sucks you under again.

Far below you, you see Sarah, her face blue in the dim underwater light, bubbles rising from her slack mouth. You dive towards her, deep into the inky blackness. Your lungs begin to burn, crying out for more air, but at last your hand clenches around Sarah's hair.

You begin to pull and kick upwards with every ounce of strength you have. You can see the sky far above you: the distant sun playing on the surface; some coloured patches that might be people leaning over the edge of the docks.

Your eardrums pop, and you realise that although you are yanking at Sarah and kicking with all your strength, you are sinking deeper, dragged down by

her weight and the weight of both of your clothes. With your free hand, you try desperately to tear some of the clothes from your body, but it is useless.

A rope! Someone has thrown a rope over the edge of the docks, and it is drifting down through the water towards you. You snatch at it, but in doing so, Sarah's hair slips from the grasp of your other hand, and she sinks out of sight into the blackness. You choke with a silent scream, and the water forces its way into your nostrils.

Someone jerks the rope upwards, and your weakened hand cannot hold on. The rope pops from your grasp. Your arms and legs windmill and kick uselessly, weakly now, until the last of your breath escapes you, and you can fight no more. Your body goes slack and sinks deeper. Your lungs fill with water. Your mind fills with dying bursts of light as you tumble down to rest on the mud at the bottom of Hobart Town's harbour.

THE END

✦ To return to your last choice and try again, go to page 233.

You take a few steadying breaths. For once, you're the calm one, and Sarah the impulsive runaway. The realisation slowly comes over you that you won't have to tell too many lies to get out of this. You can, more or less, be honest, with only a few details changed, and you'll be free.

You walk right up to Mr Tilsome and the constable, and curtsey. A few weeks of eating well at Lachlan's has returned you to a healthy weight, and your bonnet covers your cropped hair.

'This man claims you ran away from your work with him,' snarls the constable.

'I'm afraid I did, sir,' you say, humbly. 'It was the wrong thing to do, I know. I was looking for my da, but I was caught and taken to gaol.'

'I see. Go on,' says the constable sceptically.

'I spent some time in the Hobart Town gaol; then a gentleman chose me to work for him. I'm now in the employ of a Mr O'Riordan at Crayfish Point, and today I'm on an errand for him, to pick up some new robes for the parish priest.'

'She's lying!' cries Mr Tilsome, and his hand darts out and rips away the brown paper from the parcel you're carrying. He stops short when he sees the priest's robes.

'Priest's robes, just as she says,' states the constable.

'I can prove I spent my time in prison, too, sir – my hair's been cut, you see?' You pull back your bonnet. For once you're glad of your spiky shorn hair.

'Indeed it has. Very well. Mr Tilsome, I understand your anger at the girl's disappearance, but I can't arrest her. She has done her time behind bars, and is now in the employ of another man. Good day, sir.'

Your elation as you climb up into the cart to drive away is dampened when you see Sarah being led away by Mr Tilsome, who is tight-lipped with anger. Sarah looks back at you, desperately. You know how lonely she must be out in Bothwell. You miss her terribly, too. You want to run and hug her, but there's nothing you can do right now.

I'll come back for you, Sarah, you think. *One day, we'll live together as sisters again...if you'll ever forgive me for abandoning you.*

When you arrive back at Crayfish Point, flushed with triumph, Lachlan is standing in the doorway waiting for you. He has twisted one of his hankies into a knot, and he is shifting uneasily from foot to foot.

'Well done,' he says when he sees the parcel of robes. 'That's marvellous – *you're* marvellous. But now...I have news.'

'Bad news?'

'No, it's good! Well, it's both, really. Come inside. Now, before I tell you, I want you to know something: I care for you...very much. I don't want anything to happen to you...to us. Please remember that.'

'Come on, Lachlan, what is it?'

'I've had word from your father. He survived. He's nearby, and...he's a bushranger! He has a gang, and they're camped out near here. I've promised to take you to him. Do you want to go?'

'Do I want to *go*?' you squeal. 'Get into the cart this instant and get me to my da!'

As it turns out, you can't take the cart along the narrow tracks you'll need to follow, so you unhitch Lachlan's horse from the cart, and ride together on its back through the ferny undergrowth at full speed.

Your body flows with the horse's rhythm. The speed is breathtaking. You crash through streams and lean right over the horse's neck to urge him up mossy slopes. Clods of earth kick up under his feet, and clouds of horsey breath form in the cool, moist air. You see smoke through the trees.

'This is it,' says Lachlan, and in the next instant you see the canvas tents, the little campfire, and a man stepping out from behind a fallen tree, raising a musket.

'Whoa!' shouts Lachlan. 'It's us. I've brought Patrick's daughter.'

The man lowers his musket, and tugs a black handkerchief down from his face to reveal a wild auburn beard. It's Da.

He runs to you, and you let him sweep you down off the horse's back like you weigh no more than a child. He presses you to his chest. He smells of bush smoke, woollen jumpers, and a musky, familiar smell that you haven't breathed since you were thirteen years old. You don't want the hug to ever end.

He breaks away and looks at you, cups your face in his hand, his fingers rough. His voice is husky with tears.

'My darling, it's a dream come true. Just look at you. You're not a child but a young woman. Riding a horse better than most men I know – your granny Catherine was the same and would be right proud. Tell me you didn't suffer too much these last years.'

'It's all right now, Da,' you choke out. 'The thing I suffered from most was missing you.'

'And I, too. Nothing those redcoats did to me could break me, nor anything I endured on the run, for I knew I had to find you. And now I have.'

You bury your face in his chest again and let the tears overtake you. Suddenly, the part of you that has been brave for so long – that has endured your mother's death, Newgate Prison, transportation, the Hobart Town gaol, losing Sarah yet again – can finally let go. You feel safe, enveloped in love, for the first time in years. You let the feeling flood through you, and you finally feel, with Da by your side, that Van Diemen's Land is home.

Da looks up at Lachlan. 'Thank you, O'Riordan,' he says, 'for bringing my daughter to me. After today, I'll have to go on the run once more, but I hope I can send you word once or twice a year so we can meet again…'

'Once or twice a year!' you blurt. 'After all this time? Da, I don't want to spend another minute without you!'

'Nor do I without you,' he agrees. 'But I'm an

outlaw – I have to keep moving, you see. It's the noose for me if they catch me this time.'

'Then I'll come on the run with you,' you announce.

'Darling, I wouldn't put you through that. It's a tough and uncertain life – your bed a sack under a bush; your food a possum, if you can catch one; the land full of cruel men hunting you down. There's nothing romantic about it. There's another life waiting for you, a much better one.'

Da looks at Lachlan and smiles. Lachlan flushes a deep red and his voice is trembling when he next speaks.

'Mr Ryan, with your permission, I'd like to ask your daughter a question.'

Lachlan picks up a gumleaf and rolls it into a circle just the right size for a finger. He gets down on one knee, and his eyes seem to dance with reflections from the campfire. He brushes his hair aside awkwardly, and takes a deep breath.

'Will you do me the honour of giving me your hand in marriage?'

Your heart begins to pound. Lachlan gazes up at you with a nervous smile. Da gives you a wink. Time itself seems to slow down, as if your whole life has built up to this point…this decision.

You adore Lachlan, and you want to be with him always. But if you say yes to him, you will have to leave Da behind... for now, at least.

If you say no, you'd break Lachlan's heart – and your own – but you could stay with Da and join his gang.

What should you do?

✦ If you turn down Lachlan and join Da's gang, go to page 244.

✦ If you agree to marry Lachlan, go to page 247.

You feel a slow, horrible ache growing in your chest, like your heart is being split in two.

Your silence hangs in the air. The campfire crackles and pops. You see the hopefulness drain from Lachlan's face. He is still on one knee, still holding the twirled leaf in his fingertips. Your da shifts uncomfortably.

You can't bear to say the word 'no' aloud, but everyone knows what you are thinking. Lachlan gets to his feet. He can't meet your eye. He brushes the leaf litter from his knee.

'If I said yes, could you stay here, with me and Da?' you ask him weakly, already knowing the answer.

Lachlan, it seems, can't bring himself to speak. So Da answers for him: 'Lachlan's work for a free Ireland is too important to give up. He must continue – no matter what.'

Lachlan nods sadly.

You slowly shake your head.

'Darling, he's a good man—' begins your father.

'I know he is – the best I'll ever find,' you interject. 'But I can't leave you, Da. I've been chained and gaoled; you've been whipped and worked to within an inch of your life. You've climbed mountains to find me, and I've crossed oceans to find you. So many times, either one of us could have died. The fact that we haven't – that we're standing here, free and face to face...that means more to me than anything in the world right now. I can't let it go. I'm so sorry, Lachlan.' The last part comes out as a croak.

Lachlan bows to you deeply, and turns to leave. The sight of his bowed back is awful. You'd do almost anything to take the pain from him...anything except lose Da again.

Now you know why he seemed so anxious when he told you about Da. He must have been worried you'd do exactly this. The sound of his horse's hooves fades into the bush.

Da's voice breaks the pained silence. 'I'd best introduce you to the gang, then,' he says. 'They're off getting firewood.'

He sticks his fingers in his mouth and whistles piercingly. After a few minutes, six men make their

way back to the campsite, each carrying an armful of wood, eyeing you curiously.

You wipe away a tear and get ready to meet Da's gang. Lachlan's gone, and you suppose you won't see Sarah again, either. These men will now be your new friends and family...

✱ To continue with the story, go to page 207.

You look into Lachlan's kind, hopeful eyes. 'I'd be honoured to be your wife,' you tell him.

You know you're still young, but you've never felt so certain of anything before in your life. Every detail around you seems brighter than before, as if this place, its circle of trees, is etching itself into your memory for safekeeping.

'Hip, hip, hooray!' shouts Da, and an echo from the valley replies.

Hooray!

Hooray!

Hooray!

'This requires celebratory billy tea for all!' Da cries. 'And now I have so much to tell you, my darling!' He gives a shout for the rest of his gang to come and join you.

Lachlan slips the gumleaf around your finger, with a kiss on your cheek. As you're still a convict, you'll have to apply to the Lieutenant Governor for permission to marry, but after that, Lachlan promises to buy you a fine ring in Hobart Town.

You put the gumleaf into your pocket. You will keep it forever, to remind you of this day.

✦ To continue with the story, go to page 220.

Epilogue

It is thirteen years later – 1840 in Richmond, Van Diemen's Land. The hens are clucking in the yard. You're in the kitchen stirring porridge for breakfast, your bare feet cool on the flagstones. Little Catherine, still sleepy-eyed and warm, cuddles your leg as you cook, while your son Abel rushes about on the dewy grass outside among the sunshine and hens.

Your husband, Lachlan, is away in town on 'business' – really, helping another Irish political prisoner – but you're not lonely, for your dear friend Sarah was finally granted her ticket of leave, and her cottage is just down the road. Sarah and Mike's daughter loves to play with Abel and Catherine, and Sarah has another baby on the way, too.

On the rare bad days, when the weather turns foul or money runs short or rats get into the oats,

you always stop and remind yourself of how far you've come. You were only three years older than Abel is now when you were struggling for survival on the streets of London, your ma dead and your da in gaol.

The darkness and filth in Newgate Prison; the storm you survived at sea, when the foal was born; the time you found Sarah in Hobart Town gaol and persuaded the master to take her home – all of these have now become stories that your children ask to hear again and again.

You only wish your da had been here to see your children grow up – but, to your sorrow, you have not seen him these last thirteen years. There's been no word of his capture or death in the *Hobart Town Gazette*, but you believe he must have died in the bush. The Shadow Gang seems to have dispersed – at least, there's no news of their activities in the papers. Nevertheless, you include Da – or his soul – in your prayers every night.

Your son Abel may be close to the same age as you were when you lived in London, but by contrast, he is sturdy, cheeky, and can read and write well – though he'd prefer to be running wild in the bush. He rides horses bareback and catches frogs in his bare hands to show little Catherine, who is fascinated – you're proud to see she's a tough, brave little spirit, like yourself.

Suddenly Abel comes rushing through the door. 'There's an old tramp in the yard, Ma!' he cries. 'I should tell him to go away, shouldn't I, as Da's not here?'

Lachlan always tells Abel it's his job to protect his mother and sister while Lachlan is away, and the boy takes his responsibility seriously.

You frown. 'Don't do that, Abel. I'm sure he's just hungry. Fetch the bread, and I'll cut him a piece.'

The old man appears in the doorway. His face is as lined as crumpled paper, and he wears a big oilskin coat. You are surprised to see his blue eyes glistening with tears.

You step towards him, holding out the bread. 'There's food here for you, sir, if you're hungry.'

'You don't recognise me, do you?' he asks. His voice is husky, like a dry leaf. Catherine begins to cry, and you hoist her onto your hip. Your mind is a blur.

Abel's eyes grow wide. The boy is always the first to catch on, his bright mind leaps and bounds ahead of anyone else's. He squeals: 'Grandpa!' and throws himself across the room at the old man.

Your da drops to his knees and scoops up your son in a bear hug. 'How did you know it was me?' he asks, half-laughing, half-crying, running his fingers through Abel's hair. 'We've never even met!'

'I just knew!' Abel says. 'I felt it in my tummy.'

'Oh, you're a good boy,' says your da, squeezing him tight, and you run across the room and throw yourself onto the heap of your family, arms and bodies all jumbled and pressed in together.

You are kissing Abel. Da is kissing you. Catherine is being kissed by everyone, and laughing and flapping her hands.

'Welcome home,' you tell your da.

Catherine is shouting 'Gan-pa! Gan-pa!' She's quick on the uptake too.

Your da is grinning from ear to ear. Your heart is so full of gladness you think it might burst.

'Will Grandpa really live here with us now?' asks Abel.

'He will,' you tell Abel. 'Happily ever after.'

THE END

FACT FILE:
SMALLPOX

Smallpox was a highly contagious disease, which killed approximately 400,000 Europeans every year during the early 1800s.

Around sixty per cent of adults and eighty per cent of children who caught smallpox died from it, although if you had it and survived, you could never catch it again. Having someone to look after you and give you food and water while you were ill would improve your chances of survival, but many families left smallpox victims to suffer alone, for fear of becoming infected themselves.

People with smallpox experienced high fevers, strong headaches and joint pain, vomiting, and a horrible rash that covered the whole body. Some people survived smallpox but were left blind because the rash spread to their eyes and permanently damaged them.

There is still no known cure for smallpox, but luckily for us, the disease was wiped out in the 1970s by a team of doctors who travelled all around the world vaccinating people, to prevent anyone from catching it in the first place.

Other awful diseases that existed in Britain in the early 1800s that we don't often experience today included scarlet fever, typhus, diphtheria and tuberculosis. These diseases were often easily spread because of poverty and unclean living conditions.

✦ Return to page 17 to make your choice.

FACT FILE:
PICKPOCKETS

London in the early 1800s was a crowded and sometimes desperate place. A lot of people were very poor, and many children, some as young as five, were taught how to pick pockets as a way of getting some money to help them stay alive.

A common way of training pickpockets was to hang a jacket from a hook with a bell attached. You had to try to take a wallet from the coat's pocket without making the bell ring. If that sounds like a fun game, consider this: child pickpockets were usually badly treated – often beaten – by their masters, and if they were caught by the authorities, they could be sentenced to death by hanging.

Charles Dickens' book *Oliver Twist* is a famous story about a boy who becomes a pickpocket on the streets of London.

Pickpocketing does still exist today, but it isn't a common crime in Australia. Lower-income families in Australia are now given an allowance from the government, which means they don't have to steal to survive. Also, all children in Australia today must go to school, whereas in London in the 1800s, only very rich children were able to attend school, leaving many poor children on the streets.

It's interesting to think that eliminating crimes like pickpocketing has been achieved today by supporting people to live more comfortable and healthy lives, not by making the punishments for crimes even worse.

✦ Return to page 30 to make your choice.

FACT FILE:
CHILD LABOUR

In the 1800s, Europe was going through a stage of industrialisation, which means that, because of new machines that had recently been invented, things that were previously made by hand (like homespun cloth) were now made by machine.

Although children had always done some work around the home and on farms, as more factories and mines opened, children were now wanted more than ever before to do dangerous, repetitive work tending to the machines, cleaning the factories, or going down the mines.

There were no laws to protect children from working, and in the cities of Britain at that time, children usually started work at around eight years old. They made only a tiny amount of money, and they were often killed, either suddenly, by accidents with the machines or down mines, or slowly, by sicknesses brought on by inhaling coaldust or cloth fibres.

Many countries, including Australia, now have

laws that protect children from being exploited by work. (You can still do some types of work, so long as it doesn't interfere with your schooling or your development in any way. Including housework, unfortunately!)

However, in some countries – particularly those badly affected by poverty – children are still forced to work long hours under terrible conditions to support their family, just as many British children in the 1800s did.

✳ Return to page 37 to make your choice.

FACT FILE: PRISONS

Britain in the 1700s and 1800s had many problems, which all fed into each other. For a start, there were simply too many people living there. Overcrowding, and the resulting lack of affordable food and accommodation, drove many desperate people to a life of crime. Criminals were sentenced harshly - whipped, hung or locked up even for minor offences - and so soon there were not enough jails, or gaols, to hold all the criminals.

As a result, in the 1700s, Britain started transporting prisoners to colonies of the British Empire, such as Australia or America. This solved two problems, somewhat relieving overcrowding in the prison system, and also providing a workforce to build new settlements in the colonies. The American War of Independence (1775-1783) put an end to convicts being transported to America, and transportation to the Australian colonies began soon after.

Even before the American War of Independence, Britain still had too many prisoners to fit in its jails.

In 1766, parliament agreed that prisoners could be kept on prison hulks instead. It was supposed to be a two-year measure, but it lasted for eighty-two years!

Prison hulks - like the one Da is held on - were ships that had once been used by the British navy, but were no longer seaworthy. Prisoners were allowed out to work during the day, and locked into the ships at night. The hulks were vile, overcrowded, violent places. The hulk system for containing prisoners became so useful to the British authorities that hulks were also used to contain prisoners in the colonies, including Australia.

Newgate Prison was in the centre of London, next to the Old Bailey courthouse. It was in use for over seven hundred years, from 1188 to 1902, and was added onto and partially rebuilt many times. The conditions inside were overcrowded and unsanitary - the stench of the prison was so awful that passers-by held their noses. Public executions took place on the gallows outside Newgate and usually attracted huge crowds, who cheered to see condemned prisoners meet their end.

✦ Return to page 76 to make your choice.

FACT FILE:
TASMANIAN ABORIGINAL PEOPLE

Indigenous people adapted to live in all of Australia's environments, from the deserts and tropics to the snowy south. Some people believe that the First Peoples of Tasmania actually walked there over 40,000 years ago, when Lutruwita (Tasmania) and the mainland were still joined. However, the Creation stories of Tasmanian Aboriginal people tell us that they have been here forever.

Before Australia's colonisation (the invasion by white people), Tasmanian Aboriginal people lived in a number of different groups around the island, and spoke different languages. The groups traded with each other and met for ceremonies. Their knowledge of the land, of seasons, animals, food, plants and medicine was incredibly detailed, and they had – and still have – a rich and vibrant culture and spirituality.

All this came under threat from colonisation. Tasmanian Aboriginal people suffered terribly from the arrival of the colonisers. Not only did the colonisers take their lands, they also spread diseases that killed whole families, and they committed brutal and bloody massacres. Tasmanian Aboriginal people fought back strongly against this invasion to defend their lands, their families, and their way of life, but by the start of the 1830s, they had been overpowered.

The colonisers sent away those Tasmanian Aboriginal people who survived this onslaught, to live at a place white people named Wybalenna ('black man's houses') instead on Flinders Island and Cape Barren Island in the Bass Strait. The colonisers presumed these survivors would eventually all die there – and most did. Forty-seven people survived Wybalenna. In 1847, they were taken to a place south of Hobart called Oyster Cove, where they eventually died.

However, despite everything that was taken from them, the Tasmanian Aboriginal people survived through the lineage of a number of strong Aboriginal women who were taken, mostly as slaves, to islands in the Bass Strait by sealers. Today, they are passing their culture down to the next generations. They have revived and are speaking their language – palawa kani – and continue to speak up to protect their families and their beautiful homeland, Lutruwita (Tasmania).

✢ Return to page 149 to make your choice.

FACT FILE:
WHAT HAPPENED TO WAYLITJA'S PEOPLE?

In this book, Waylitja (pronounced 'why-lee-tcha') is a fictional Tasmanian Aboriginal boy, whose family lives around the area named by colonisers as Bothwell, in the broader region known as Big River.

Theresa Sainty is a Tasmanian Aboriginal Elder, who chose Waylitja's name for this book and can tell us more about the story of his people. palawa kani is the revived form of the original Tasmanian Aboriginal languages. It's a combination of words from many of the original Tasmanian Aboriginal languages. Theresa herself is one of the language workers who revived palawa kani.

EMILY: What does Waylitja's name mean, and why did you choose it?

THERESA: 'Waylitja' is the palawa kani word for a parrot. palawa kani is the revived Tasmanian Aboriginal language, and the only Tasmanian Aboriginal language now spoken here in Lutruwita.

So when I was thinking about what we might call this young man, I thought of Waylitja, because of what he talks about in the book in terms of birds and animals. He's got a lot of knowledge of all the resources that are within his country, and I thought that was a really nice name. I imagined that it could have been the name of one of our ancestors in the past.

And it's an Oyster Bay/Big River word, and Bothwell either falls within, or is on the edge of, what we now know as Big River country, and so that was another reason why I thought that would be a good name for him.

EMILY: Waylitja's people were the Big River people. What would their lives have been like before the invasion of white people?

THERESA: We know those old fellas would have spent the summer – well, what we now call summer – in their own country. But during the colder part of the year, those people had an arrangement with the Oyster Bay people on the east coast, so they would come down from the very cold lakes area and spend the colder times on the coast.

They were pretty lucky. They had rainforest-type resources, like the plants, foods and the animals, and the freshwater fish in the river systems, and then they came down to the coast and were able to feast on things like mutton-birds and shellfish.

EMILY: In one of the scenes in the book, Waylitja gives a shell necklace as a gift. Can you say a few words about the significance of shell necklaces, and perhaps how he would have come to have one?

THERESA: Shell necklaces are one of the oldest traditions, not just here in Tasmania but, really, worldwide, because it is a living tradition – Tasmanian Aboriginal people continue to make shell necklaces.

I imagine that when the Big River Mob went down to the coast, even if they didn't make the necklaces themselves, they were possibly traded. So that's one way he may have come by one.

EMILY: In the book, Waylitja leaves, and at that time the reader doesn't understand why, and doesn't see him again. Considering the historical knowledge we now have, why do you think Waylitja's family left, and what would have happened to them next?

THERESA: Well, most of the original people no longer exist, as a result of settlers murdering them, massacres, introduced diseases and probably even not being able to reach their food, because as white people came the country was carved up.

The white people came in, built their houses and farms and brought their livestock, and put up fences. So, areas that our people had kept healthy by fire, which encouraged new growth, which encouraged the animals to come in to feed - hunting grounds, which had been so carefully looked after for many generations - were not accessible to them, because now there were farms in the middle of them. They had been pushed out.

Of course, there was also the war that our people were fighting for country. So those people who weren't killed off by those different things that we talked about...they were fighting trying to drive white people off their country. They didn't give up country without a fight, and so towards the end, Big River people and the Oyster Bay people – the remnants of those groups – joined together, and they were fighting together as one group.

In the end, the settlers took the remainder of our people to Flinders Island. In the Great Lakes area, the remnants of Waylitja's people met with Robinson*, and agreed to go with him for a time. Around 17th January 1835, there's a description from a white person's perspective of them marching through the streets of Hobart, and from there they were shipped off to Wybalenna on Flinders Island, and they never saw their country again, because most people died at Wybalenna.

So, maybe Waylitja was fighting the war with his people, I don't know. But the fact of

---

* George Augustus Robinson was employed by the government of Van Dieman's Land. He promised the surviving Tasmanian Aboriginal people that the settlement called Wybalenna on Flinders Island would be a place where they could practise their culture in freedom, but conditions at Wybalenna were more like a prison camp, and the population suffered greatly from disease and homesickness.

the matter is, he would have died. If he didn't die from fighting for country, or if he wasn't massacred, he was eventually taken to Wybalenna.

✦ Return to page 172 to continue with the story.

FACT FILE:
CONVICTS IN VAN DIEMEN'S LAND

All of the convicts who arrived in Van Diemen's Land (as Tasmania was known then) were put straight to work, either as servants for free men, or in gangs doing physical labour like mining coal, cutting stone, or felling trees. A lot of hard work and a lot of resources were needed for the growing colony to become established.

The life of a convict was tough, but many convicts who were prepared to work hard and obey the rules managed to make a new life for themselves after they gained their freedom. Others, however, were abused by their masters; tried to escape and were punished; or became involved in further crime once they reached Van Diemen's Land.

We often hear mention today of convicts who were transported to the Australian colonies for simply 'stealing a loaf of bread'. Along with these, however, were other convicts who were genuinely violent and hardened criminals.

Penal settlements were established and jails were built in the colonies to contain and manage troublesome convicts. The jails for women were sometimes known as 'female factories' and were smaller and closer to town. The jails for men were larger, and most were situated in more isolated penal settlements that were difficult to escape from, such as Port Arthur and Macquarie Harbour.

These places in particular had a reputation for being hell on earth. Convicts were forced to do long, exhausting days of gruelling physical work, with barely enough food or clothing to keep them alive, and they were whipped or put into isolation cells for disobedience.

Convicts at times became so desperate that they preferred to die than to continue life in one of these penal settlements. Some of these convicts tried to escape, and died in the wilderness or were shot while escaping. Others murdered another convict or an officer in plain view of witnesses, knowing that the penalty for murder was death, but seeing this as a preferable option to the never-ending suffering of servitude.

✦ Return to page 179 to continue with the story.

FACT FILE: MATTHEW BRADY

During the fifty years that Britain transported 75,000 convicts to Tasmania, four hundred escaped convicts took up arms and became bushrangers. This was one of the highest rates of rebellion in any of the British colonies.

Matthew Brady was an English convict, who was sent to Sydney on a seven-year sentence in 1820. He rebelled against the harsh conditions of convict labour in Sydney and was repeatedly given 'the lash' for attempting escape. Eventually, Brady was sent as punishment to the newly created penal station of Sarah Island, in Macquarie Harbour, Van Diemen's Land, in 1823.

In 1824, Brady and some other men managed to steal a small boat and make their escape from Macquarie Harbour. They then began their life as bushrangers in Van Diemen's Land. Brady became known as the Gentleman Bushranger by his admirers, as he was so well-mannered while robbing his victims, and in particular treated ladies very politely.

The government was not impressed and put up posters advertising a reward for his capture. In return, Brady put up posters advertising a reward of twenty gallons of rum in return for the capture of Governor Arthur!

After nearly two years as bushrangers in Van Diemen's Land, Brady and his gang captured a boat, planning to sail it to the Australian mainland, but were forced to turn back due to bad weather.

Eventually, Brady was betrayed by one of his gang members, who led the soldiers to him in return for a pardon.

Brady was hanged to death in 1826. His cell was filled with flowers from many ladies of Hobart, who had adored and admired the Gentleman Bushranger.

✦ Return to page 202 to make your choice.

FACT FILE:
Irish Political Prisoners in Van Diemen's Land

Ever since Ireland joined the United Kingdom in the year 1800, there have been those who have wanted independence and freedom for Ireland. There have been many wars fought for Irish independence, but to this day it remains part of the United Kingdom.

Some Irish rebels were sent to Australia as convicts – including to Van Diemen's Land. Da's act of rebellion (burning an English vessel) saw him transported and treated as a common criminal. However, other political prisoners were sometimes revolutionary journalists and politicians arrested for 'treason' – betrayal of one's country (which in this case was England, not Ireland). Many of them were well-educated and from wealthy families. Because of this, and because they had not committed violent crimes, they tended to be treated better than regular convicts by the authorities.

One well-known group of fifteen Irish political

prisoners sent to Van Diemen's Land, in 1849, were part of a group who called themselves the Young Irelanders. Their leader, William Smith O'Brien, was originally sentenced to death for treason – however, his sentence was lessened to transportation to Australia after 17,000 people in the United Kingdom signed petitions begging for him not to be killed.

Some people who supported Irish independence came to Australia voluntarily, as free settlers, with the aim of helping Irish political prisoners, especially leaders from the movement, to escape the country, which was illegal. In this book, Lachlan O'Riordan is a fictional example of one of these people. They took great personal risks to support their leaders and help their cause.

✦ Return to page 233 to make your choice.

DID THAT REALLY HAPPEN?

Although I've had help from historians to check facts in this book, I'm first and foremost a storyteller. When I found interesting bits of history, I wanted to include them, even if it meant taking some poetic licence. Here are a few points of clarification, as well as some interesting connections to my own family's past...

The bracelet in the hem of the petticoat...

NOT LIKELY, BUT POSSIBLE. Convicts were provided with new clothes at the start of their voyage. They were also thoroughly searched, scrubbed down, and if their old clothes were tattered, these were incinerated. So there would have been lots of opportunities for your bracelet to be found and taken from you, but if your petticoat was in good condition, and if no one noticed the treasure in your hem when they were searching you, you may have managed to keep it. Convicts who were transported

were allowed to keep personal items with them. 'Acrostic' jewellery, where each gemstone stands for a letter spelling a secret message, did exist and was a popular fashion throughout the 1800s.

Meeting your end at the hands of a murderous doctor...

YES AND NO. Doctors and medical researchers in Britain in the early 1800s needed to use human corpses for dissection to better understand the workings of human bodies. Medical schools paid good money for dead bodies, which led to the awful practice of graverobbers digging up freshly buried bodies to sell for a profit. Some graverobbers went even further and started murdering the victims themselves, but their crimes were discovered when medical schools became suspicious. There is no evidence that doctors themselves ever colluded in these murders, or wanted live subjects for experimentation. That part of the story is pure fiction.

The house at Bothwell, the bushrangers, and the arson attack...

YES, BUT THE DATES HAVE BEEN ALTERED. The Tilsomes' house in Bothwell is based on Sherwood, my ancestors' property, although my ancestors lived in a log cabin at first and their sandstone house wasn't built until the late 1830s. The sandstone quarry that you fall into in the story is real, as was the arson attack by local Aboriginal people in retaliation for the theft of their land, and did not occur until 1830, not long after a shepherd on the same property was speared to death. The bushrangers' attack also occurred at Sherwood, though not until 1843. It was led by Martin Cash and his gang, who really did give the master's tobacco and alcohol to the servants! Although a young girl joining a bushranging gang is fiction, there are accounts of one or two women bushrangers.

The friendship with Waylitja...

UNLIKELY, BUT NOT IMPOSSIBLE. Amid the violence and dispossession, there are records of colonisers treating Tasmanian Aboriginal people with kindness. Colonisers of the Quaker faith, such as Dr George Story and the Cotton family, befriended Aboriginal people on the east coast of Tasmania and sheltered them from attacks. Throughout Australia's colonised history, there have been hundreds, if not thousands, of people who rose above what society expected of them and formed friendships, alliances and romantic partnerships across racial divides. We can only hope that in Van Diemen's Land in this era, in our story, it would have been possible for you to do so too.

A young convict girl being assigned to a single male master...

NO, NOT AT THIS TIME. It was actually against regulations for a young female convict to be assigned to a single male master (such as Mr Tilsome before his family comes, or Lachlan). This was to protect the young women from potentially predatory men. However, I decided it was in the best interests of the plot to keep those parts in.

The Irish political prisoners escaping Van Diemen's Land...

YES, BUT NOT UNTIL DECADES LATER. Again, this is based on my own family history: my husband's family, the Conolans, had an ancestor called Bernard Conolan who came to Tasmania to assist Irish political prisoners to escape Van Diemen's Land. (And indeed, one was disguised in a priest's outfit!) However, this happened later than is shown in the book, in 1853. My husband has inherited a large amethyst ring, sent from America to Bernard Conolan as a gift of thanks from John Mitchel, the political prisoner he helped to freedom. But as the fight for Ireland's independence from England goes back to the year 1800, I think there always would have been Irish rebels like Da in the Australian colonies, as well as those who wished to assist them.

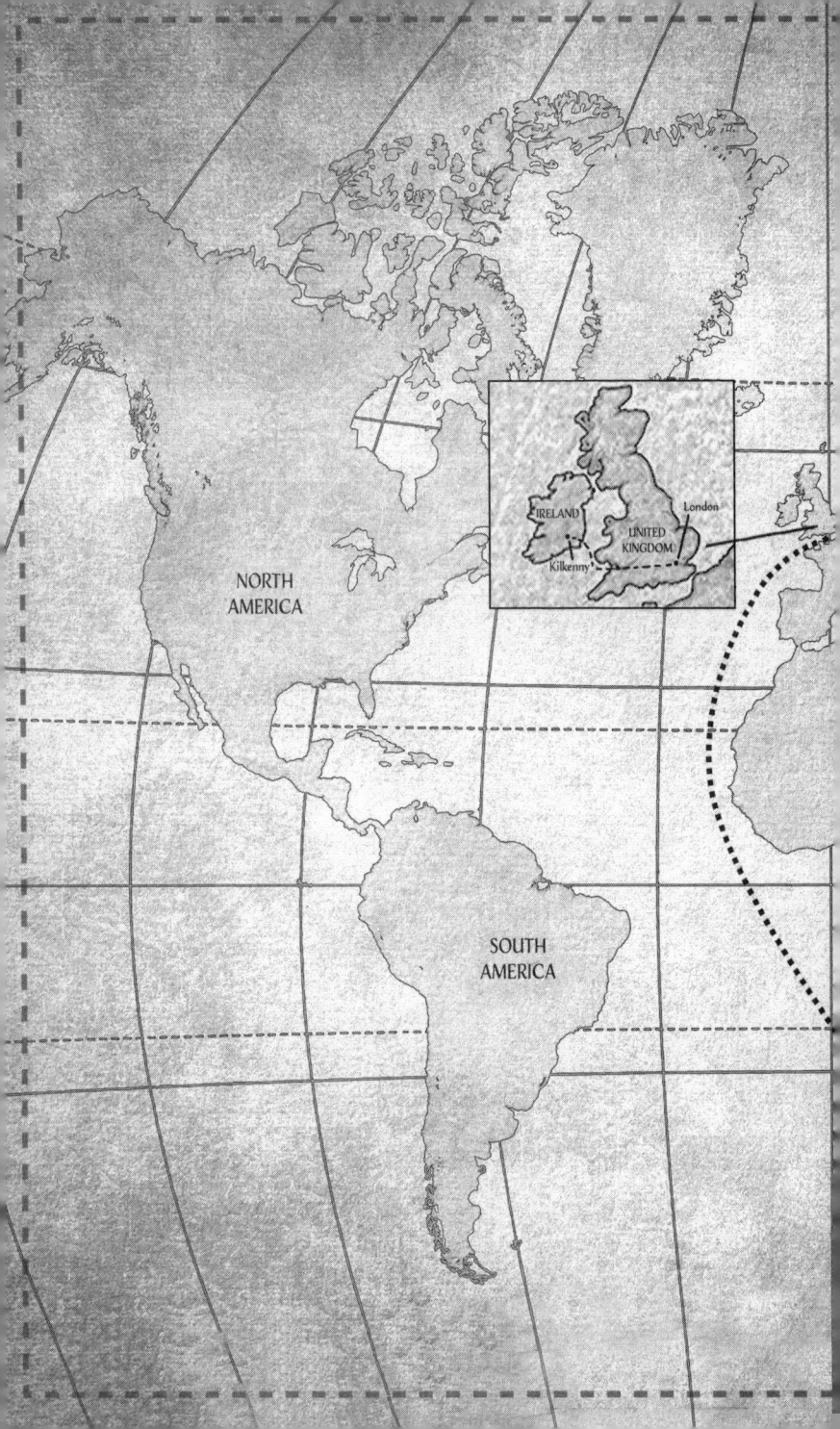

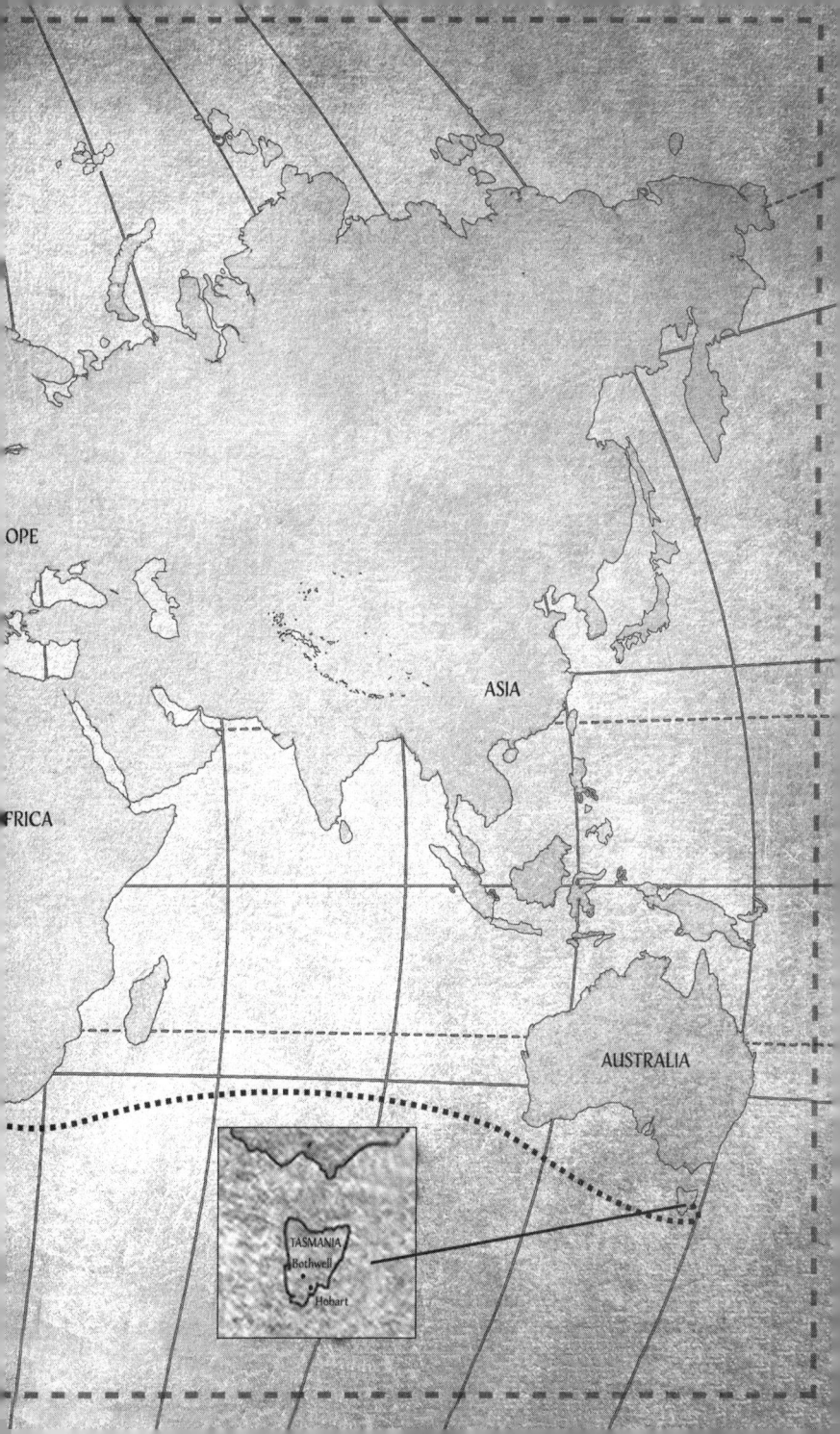

Acknowledgements

I WAS LUCKY to be born into a world where books and reading were everywhere. When I was four or five, I remember my dad complaining about the cats getting into the garbage bin, and I suggested writing a sign asking them to stay away. When my dad informed me that cats *couldn't read*, I was shocked and felt sorry for them – in my world, everyone and everything that was alive could read, just like we all made sounds and moved. So, my acknowledgements begin with my mum, who taught me to read, the rest of my family (especially Dad, Lissy and Annie), my teachers, my school librarian, and the authors of so many marvellous children's books, who helped a bookworm like me take such joy in words, and never stop.

The journey to publication has been complex and wonderful, and many people have helped. Erica Wagner is my publisher (I still get a kick out of saying the words 'my publisher'!), who saw the potential in the Freedom Finders, championed it into reality, and gave rock-solid advice and deep kindness.

Elise Jones is my editor, who has been like a wonderful dance partner – responsive, enthused, aware and communicative. She cares about this series as much as I do, and her dedication shows everywhere on these pages. (I'd show you a first draft by way of comparison, but that would be too embarrassing.)

The rest of the team at Allen & Unwin have been so excited by the series and committed to its success; I couldn't have asked for better support.

Stephen Mushin gets a special shout-out for being a genie-skull who always has my back, comes up with the best ideas, and encourages me to shoot for the stars. Sher Rill Ng has produced amazingly lush cover art for the series, which I just love. Hamish Maxwell-Stewart and Rebecca Read at the University of Tasmania were terrific at spotting details where my imagination had coloured outside the lines of actual historical fact.

My great thanks and respect also go to Ruth Langford, Tony Burgess, Tony Brown, Denise Robinson, Lisa Fuller and, especially, Theresa Sainty, who generously made time to discuss and enrich the Tasmanian Aboriginal cultural content in this book, and to the Tasmanian Aboriginal Corporation, who approved the use of the palawa kani word 'Waylitja'.

Caitlin Barratt, Keeley Jones, and Mr Jeffery's Grade 5/6 class of 2016 were all great guinea-pig readers in the early days. Lola Conolan piqued my interest in Conolan family history and the Irish rebels of Van Diemen's Land; I was so touched when she read an early draft and told me that she loved my fictionalised portrayal of Bernard Conolan. I treasure the time we had together, and wish we could have more. Deep love and gratitude also to my Mamabake friends and everyone else who listened, made cups of tea, and became the proverbial village it takes to raise two children and a book series.

My husband, Matt, is my bedrock and life partner in every way, including being the dad of Anwen and Ben, who fill me with oodles of love. Lastly, thank *you*, dear reader, because there would have been no point in writing this book at all if it weren't for your readiness to read it. (I'm only sorry that no cats ever will.)

About the Author

EMILY CONOLAN IS a writer and teacher, who is also known for her humanitarian work. For her role in establishing a volunteer support network for asylum seekers in Tasmania, she has been awarded Tasmanian of the Year, Hobart Citizen of the Year, and the Tasmanian Human Rights Award. The stories of courage and resilience she has heard in the course of her work with refugees, combined with tales from her own family history, inspired her to write the Freedom Finders series.